WISTFUL

THE TRUTH IS EVERYONE IS GOING TO HURT YOU. YOU JUST GOT TO FIND THE ONES WORTH SUFFERING FOR.

Bob Marley

WISTFUL

MICHAEL EDWIN Q.

Wistful by Michael Edwin Q.
Copyright © 2020 by Michael Edwin Q.
All Rights Reserved.
ISBN: 978-1-59755-563-0

Published by: ADVANTAGE BOOKS™
                  Longwood, Florida, USA
                  www.advbookstore.com

Library of Congress Catalog Number: 2020934686
1. Fiction: African American - Woman
2. Fiction: African American – Historical
3. Social Science - Slavery

Cover Design: Judith San Nocolas
Editor: nancysabitinicopyedit@gmail.com

First Printing: March 2020
20 21 22 23 24 25   10 9 8 7 6 5 4 3 2 1
Printed in the United States of America

Michael Edwin Q.

Only one letter separates the two words
Wishful is having hope for something
Wistful is regret for what might have been

One

The Greatest Sin

He wanted them dead! He swore to kill every last one of them without mercy, but not until they suffered as he had suffered.

There was much to learn from the war being fought at the time. Like a tiny insect stinging a huge grizzly bear – one quick sting, then fly away, only to return later when their guard was down. Small military groups would attack larger groups in this manner.

That was the plan. To live and hide in the wilderness, now and then swoop down onto the plantation, causing havoc, and then killing them off one by one.

It was a one-man campaign, his only purpose in life. It didn't matter if they caught and killed him. His life was over, anyway. Everything stolen from him – freedom, love, hope, he would steal from them. In the end, as they had taken his life, he would take theirs.

****

"What is the greatest sin in the world?" Pastor Jefferies bellowed from the pulpit.

The congregation looked up in wide-eyed wonder, hanging on every word.

All the slaves from the surrounding plantations would attend Sunday service.

When Pastor Jefferies asked for permission from the landowners to erect a small church, they met him with rejection and threats. However, after further consideration, he received permission. As well, all slaves were given half a day off from work each Sunday to attend. This was not out of compassion, nor religious obligation. The plantation owners realized that without a spark of hope in life, as false as it might be, there was no controlling a slave. As well, Pastor Jefferies agreed to always preach nonviolence, which he did.

Still, every so often the owners would send someone to listen in on his sermons. It so happened that this one particular Sunday, Fergus Malum sent one of his overseers to stand outside and listen to the sermon.

When no one answered, Pastor Jefferies repeated, "What is the greatest sin in the world?" One or two of the younger members were about to respond when he added, "It's not what you think!"

The worshippers turned to stone, staring up in silence.

"It is theft!" he announced to every one's surprise. "To pridefully take from another, be it God or man, what is rightfully theirs.

"One might assume the greatest theft to be murder. But it's not. It is slavery.

"Murder takes away your life, everything you are and have. Slavery does the same only you remain alive – a witness to your lose – a lifetime of dehumanization. This is far crueler.

"Still, no matter how deep the sorrow, there is a spark of the infinite in each of us, rising to the surface, like a bubble, grasping what little joy it can, finding its place in the sun.

"Despite their lot, slaves live, love, marry, and have children, seeking a meaningful life. We must fight at every turn, or we will not survive."

The overseer heard enough, he couldn't wait to rush back to the Malum Plantation to tell his boss what he heard.

****

"Behave yourself!" she said, giggling, gently removing his hand.

Only recently, they took to serious hugging and kissing. However, a young man's passion starts as a spark that easily develops into a bonfire. Hugging and kissing only wets his appetite for more.

"Anthony, please, stop!" she said, still in a friendly tone, only more firmly.

"Why?" he asked, rising off her, his outstretched arms held him in a hovering position over her. "What does it matter? We'll marry soon."

"It matters to me," she replied, pushing him out of the way, working up onto her feet. "Besides, they'll be counting the months from our wedding day to the first baby."

Anthony's eyes went narrow. Children were not in his thoughts and plans. Still, it needed consideration.

She brushed herself off. "That reminds me . . ."

"Yeah, I know," he agreed, knowing the question without it being asked.

"How we ever gonna get married, if we don't tell our parents?"

She had a point. Not one he wanted to think about, still, a good point.

"They'll say we're too young," Anthony argued.

"I'm older than when my momma married," she countered. She thought for a moment, and then looked solemnly. "Our parents never ever talk. I don't even know if they like one another."

"My folks are sure gonna like you," he said, putting his arms around her, pullin her close.

"Oh, Anthony, I love you so much," she whispered, her head pressed against his chest. "We'll tell our folks, tonight."

"All right, tonight," he agreed.

"Promise…?"

"I promise…"

"Cross your heart and hope to die?"

"Cross my heart and hope to die."

They kissed one last time, walking back to the slave quarters. Their hands entwined, slowly breaking away as they parted.

****

Emma Pearl Tucker was seventeen and beautiful. With ribbons in her hair, sweet and petite, a tintype of her mother. Bright and sweet as peaches and cream, as girls are meant to be. With a winning smile and nature that everyone loved. Dozens of boys pursued her, except her heart was spoken for. It belonged to no one else other than Anthony.

Anthony Watson was nearing eighteen, handsome with his mother's good looks, tall and strong. From thirteen to eighteen, he grew like a tree till he was a head above all the others, a muscular body from years of working in the fields. A levelheaded young man with his feet planted firm on the ground.

Emma and Anthony never paid much attention to each other until they were in their midteens. This was strange, as they worked in the same fields and lived in the same slave quarters all their lives. Though maybe not so strange, seeing how their parents never had anything to do with one another. There was no bad blood between them. They just ignored the other, seldom speaking a word, even at church. Emma and Anthony swore that would all change.

All their friends admitted they made a beautiful couple. Even Reverend Jefferies approved. Although, when the two confronted him about setting a date for a wedding, he turned them down.

"You two got it all backwards. First, you tell your parents, and then you come to me to set a date, not the other way around."

They looked forlorn at the minister, knowing he was right, only wishing he wasn't.

"Listen," Jefferies continued, "marriage is the most grownup thing you'll ever do in your life. So, you better start acting like adults from the start. Grow up and go tell your folks, and then come back to me." He waited for the thought to sink in. "Honor your father and your mother, that your days may be long upon the land, which the Lord your God is giving you."

They looked at him with questioning looks.

Reverend Jefferies sight, "It means that if you honor your parents you'll have a long, happy, married life, and your kids won't be brats."

****

There was nothing outstanding about the Malum Plantation. It was just one of many cotton plantations in the South. Still, it was well-known in the county for its high output of product. This was mostly because of Fergus Malum keeping a tight grip around the throats of his slaves. When things ran smoothly, you never so much as heard from him. However, the slightest infraction was met with unspeakable torture and quite often death. Fergus' theory was to make an example of whoever didn't do as they were told. Keep them in fear, and you keep them in line. Even when the war broke out with the North, when most plantations experienced a decrease in productivity, Fergus hammered down all the harder. Insuring profits remained the same.

As a young man, Fergus started in the slave trade, buying and selling. He knew the business like the back of his hand. By the time he was thirty, he was a wealthy man. Wanting to live a simpler life, he bought seven hundred acres of prime farmland. In no time, he had the most profitable plantation in the county. In the center of the property he constructed a large mansion, superior in every way to neighboring plantations. Having wealth and power, the only thing missing in his life was a family.

For two years, Fergus courted and wooed every single woman at church. He was looking for more than beauty, a soul mate with like-mindedness was just as important. Estella Page, the daughter of a wealthy politician, fit the bill. She was not only beautiful; she was as racist and cruel as he. A match made in hell.

Their marriage went through a dark period. Try as they may, they were unable to have children. A male heir was crucial to Fergus' life plan. They prayed and donated large sums to the church, still, they remained childless. Oddly enough, it wasn't till they gave up all hope, and Fergus denounced all belief in God, that Estella came into the family way.

Fergus was by no means a praying man. Although, in the case of fathering a son, he'd make an exception, of course he told no one. He prayed for two years, nothing. In his discouragement, he assumed there either wasn't a god, or if there was he was powerless or uncaring, or both. So, he denounced god. Strangely enough, that was the moment Estella became pregnant. For Fergus, this confirmed his decision to be godless. Morals would no longer apply to him. He would live his life only to please himself and his family. Many atheists argue God is not necessary to be moral. They're confusing morality with accepted behavior, which can change. Whatever, Fergus believed it no longer applied to him. Still, it was good business to remain a parishioner of the local church.

It was an easy birth, which was a foreshowing of what the child would be like. They named him Douglas, after Estella's father. A beautiful baby, a lovely child, and who grew to be a handsome young man. He never wanted for anything. To say he was spoiled was an understatement. As for Douglas, the apple didn't fall far from the tree. In fact, he was more hateful than his parents. He was feared by everyone, especially the slaves of his father.

When the war between the North and South broke out, Fergus feared for his only child. He spent thousands of dollars to have his son exempt from military service. However, Douglas was determined to enlist. Fergus was unwavering in saving his son from himself.

One particular Sunday, Fergus told his son that his mother was too ill to attend church, and he would remain at her bedside. This left Douglas with only one option. He would ride into town and go to service, alone.

Fergus made arrangements with three hooligans from the next county. Their orders were to rob Douglas and to physically hurt him. Not kill him, of course, but perhaps break a bone or two, anything that would leave him incapable of becoming a soldier. It went better than planned. In his struggle with the three, Douglas' right arm was pulled out of the socket. Somehow, he made it home in great pain. The shoulder was set. In time, it healed to the point of not being in pain, yet, for the rest of his life he would never be able to raise his arm above his head without it dislocating. He could never truly be a fighting man.

"I'm so sorry, father," he told his parents. He was nearly in tears. "I wanted to make you both so proud of me."

"We are proud of you, son," Estella insured him.

"I feel I've let you down."

"It wasn't your fault, son," Fergus replied. "It couldn't be helped. It's all in God's hands." Such a strange remark for an unbeliever such as Fergus, still, Fergus believed he'd done the moral thing. He'd saved the life of his son.

****

Monk was a short, thin, unkempt, unshaven, weasel of a man. He would do anything for money, which is why Fergus hired him. Of course he never trusted him, yet as long as the money was there, Monk was faithful.

Fergus was blunt. "So, what did you learn?"

Monk wasn't going to pass up a chance to sing his own praises. "I went down to the colored church, like ya told me to. I kept low; they didn't see me. I heard every word."

"What did you hear?" Fergus insisted.

"Well, first they sang hymns. Not the kind ya hear in a real church."

"I don't care what the hell they sang," Fergus shouted. "I want to know what was said."

"Well, the preacher, he was talking kind of weird."

"Weird…what do you mean weird?"

"The pastor was sayin' things against slavery. He got `em all riled up."

Fergus looked out the window, his back to Monk. "Maybe, it's time we paid the Reverend Jefferies a visit."

Two

Understand

It was a small one-room shack in the slave quarters, made to feel smaller now that Anthony grew to be a young man.

Edna and Armand Watson loved their son, Anthony. They knew it would only be a short time before he came to them announcing he was in love. They saw the change when he turned seventeen. Not only in the way he began looking at young women, but in the way they began to eye him. An announcement of marriage would not be a surprise. Although, a declaration of love for Emma Pearl Tucker was not met with the enthusiasm that Anthony hoped for. Although, at first his father seemed keen on the idea, it was his mother who protested.

Edna was a wise old woman; she understood life, men, and her son. She knew if she came right out saying "no", putting her foot down, Anthony would only rebel. Subtle questions at first, then work upward.

"You're both a bit young, don't you think? Especially, her...?"

"She's sixteen. You and Papa were married in your teens, so were her parents."

"I mean in maturity. She doesn't seem mature, yet."

"How would you know," Anthony said firmly, "You've never talked to her."

"Come to think of it," Armand added, "We've never talked with any of the Tucker family." He turned to his wife. "Why is that, Edna? They seem like nice enough people."

She ignored him, continuing, "There are so many other young women on the plantation. Better catches, if you ask me."

"I don't know," Armand put in, "Emma seems like a nice enough girl."

Again, his wife him. This time, Anthony couldn't help but notice.

"Anthony," his mother began, "if you marry this girl, your life will be ruined. Believe me."

"How can you say that? You don't even know Emma."

"Oh, I know her. I know the type of person she is. I grew up around her kind. She acts like a good girl in front of you. But she'll stab you in the back, as soon as look at you. She will never be faithful to you. She's a cheap slut!"

Edna jumped from subtle to warnings, and to downright rude. Anthony could take no more, jumping to his feet. Surprisingly to Anthony, his father did, also, standing in protest at this son's side.

Armand pointed his finger, pointed his finger at his wife as he spoke, "Now, Edna, you're not being fair. Hear the boy out."

"She's a cheap slut, I tell you," Edna instead once more.

"I won't have you talking that way about the woman I love," Anthony proclaimed

"Love! What do you know about love? You're still just a pup," Edna stated.

" I'm going to marry Emma, no matter what you think," he shouted, storming out.

"You'll be sorry!" she hollered at the door, after he slammed it.

When they were alone, Armand shot a questioning look at Edna. "Why did you do that?"

"I don't want to talk about this, Armand. You don't understand."

"Then help me understand."

Edna stood up, walked to the stove to prepare supper, her back to him. Armand rushed out the door, in hopes of talking with Anthony. The lad was nowhere to be found.

****

The slave village was a sad place to live. Each family got a tiny shack to live in; they were all rundown. Many folks did the best they could to fix them up, but time was the enemy. When your days are spent sweating in the fields from sunup to sundown and the rest of you day is spend trying to put food on the table, little changes.

The shack the Tuckers lived in on the other side of the slave quarters was no larger or better than the Watson's, nor that of any other family in the slave quarters. The one difference was they hung a sheet from the ceiling, encircling Emma's bed. A young woman needs her privacy.

Other than saying Grace, the family seldom spoke during supper, which was why Emma having anything say grabbed their attention.

"I have something important to tell you both," Emma announced.

Her parents, Cora and Simon, stopped eating, giving her their full attention.

"What is it, pumpkin?" Cora asked.

A long moment passed for her to drum up the courage. She took in a deep breath and held it. "I'm in love," she blurted out, exhaling slowly.

Another moment of silence, Cora stared at her daughter in disbelief. Then the moment passed, and her mother smiled with approval, though there was a look of apprehension.

A smile appeared on Simon's face.

"That's great, dear! Who's the lucky boy?" Simon asked, slowly tripping over his words.

"Anthony Watson…he's asked me to marry him."

Cora's disposition changed in the blink of an eye, as did the atmosphere. Cora laughed, "But you're only still a child…a baby!"

"I'm older than you were when you married papa."

"Times were different then," Cora reached out, placing her hand on her daughter's. "Listen to me. I understand the feelings that start up in a young girl. These feelings can only blind you from the truth. You're far too young, and this boy is not for you."

"Why not…?" Simon asked to the surprise of his wife and the gratification of his daughter.

"Are you against me, too?" Cora snapped at him.

"No one's against you, Cora. But Emma's right. She is old enough." He turned, addressing Emma. "But there are things about this whole thing I don't like. I'm your father, I deserve respect. You don't just drop this in my lap, and tell me how it's going to be. Now, Anthony seems like a nice young man, but I don't know this boy. I need to meet him, talk with him, and maybe, just maybe…then I'll give my approval. As well, if he wants to marry my daughter, he needs to ask me for her hand. That is only proper."

"Oh, Papa, you'll love him as much as I do."

"That won't be necessary. But I would like to meet him. Invite him for dinner one night next week."

Emma leaped across the table, throwing her arms around her father, kissing his cheek. "Oh, Papa, you're wonderful." Unable to contain herself, she ran for the door. "I'm going to tell Anthony, right now."

Alone, Cora confronted Simon with strong looks of disapproval.

"What?" he asked in deference.

"You have no idea what you've set in motion," Cora proclaimed.

"I just want to meet the boy. I'm not agreeing to anything, at this time."

"Simon, you don't understand. It's all going to explode in our faces."

He chuckled. "I don't know what you problem is? I wish I knew. I love you, Cora, trust me, just this once."

For a moment, Cora seemed to submit, except not fully. "Simon, you have no idea what is ahead. Turn back, for God's sake. In God's name…turn back."

"Cora, you're makin' a big thing outta nothin'. I just want to talk with the boy. I'm not going to giving my approval; I just want to be able to figure this all out."

"It's going to be a nightmare," Cora responded.

"I don't' understand you," was all Simon could say.

****

"Wait here," Fergus ordered Monk, who then sat down on the steps of the church. Fergus opened the doors and entered.

Pastor Jefferies stood at the front the pulpit, holding a paintbrush. He was in his work clothes.

"Doin' some repairs?" Fergus shouted as he walked to the front of the church.

Jefferies spun around in shock, "Mr. Malum, what a surprise. How can I help you, sir?" He placed the paintbrush down. "The pulpit needed a new coat of paint," he explained.

"That's what I came to talk to you about, Jefferies, about the pulpit…that is."

Jefferies looked puzzled.

"Sit down, Jefferies, we need to talk," Fergus said, sitting down in the first pew, the pastor sat down next to him.

"What about the pulpit, sir?"

Fergus let out a long sigh. "You like it here, Jefferies?" He didn't wait for an answer. "We pretty much let you do what you want, don't we? Do you remember our agreement?" Again, he didn't give the pastor time to answer. "You can say anything you want as long as you help keep the peace."

Jefferies looked stunned. "I've never preached anything other than keeping the peace."

"I realized that," Fergus replies. "You just need to watch what you say. There are certain things that might be misunderstood or misinterpreted. I don't want you to ever use the word *slavery*, again, ever."

"Mr. Malum, I…"

"I don't want to hear a word from you," Fergus demanded, holding one finger up in front of his lips to make his point. Jefferies went silent. Fergus continued, "You know what I'm talking about. Don't play games with me. Now, I'm going to ask you one more time. You like it here, Jefferies?"

"Yes, sir, I do."

"Save many souls, do you?"

"I can only hope so, sir."

"Good! Just remember, stay in the spiritual realm. Save as many souls as you like. Never, mention anything else. You understand, Jefferies?"

"Yes, sir, I understand."

"That's good." Fergus stood up. "And Jefferies, I will have one of my men listen in from time to time. If I'm not pleased with what you're preaching, I will see to it myself that you are stopped. That doesn't mean kicking you out of your church and send you packing. It means burning this tinderbox of a church down to the ground and scattering the ashes to the wind. And you know what I'll us to start the fire?"

Pastor Jefferies was afraid to answer.

"You…I'll use you. I'll set you on fire, and use you like a match. There will never be another black church in this county. Every Sunday will become just another workday for the coloreds. And you, Pastor Jefferies, will become a memory. Do I make myself clear?"

There was no need for the reverend to answer. His eyes told the full story, as he nodded.

"Good! You have a blessed day, Reverend," Fergus said, walking to the door and out.

Monk jumped to his feet, following Fergus.

"Monk, I want you to listen in every Sunday. Report everything you hear. Do you understand?"

"Yes, sir, I understand."

"Good!"

Three

Without Turmoil

Emma waited on the porch for Anthony. The moment he approached, she ran to him. He held and kissed her, both of them not caring who saw.

"Anthony, listen, I need to tell you some things, before we step inside."

He looked at her squarely, still holding her.

She began, "My mother is strongly against this. I don't know why."

"My mother, too, but I think my father actually likes the idea."

"My father, too," Emma replied, "except, he's mad as a wet hen about how we're doing this."

"What do you mean?"

"He didn't like me springing this on him, all at once. That's why you're here. He wanted you to come for dinner, so he can get to know you. Then, he expects you to ask for my hand. If he likes you, he'll say *yes*."

"And if he doesn't?"

"He'll like you, how can he not?" she smiled up at him.

"And your mother…?"

"I don't know. Just watch what you say?" She gently broke free from his arms. Placing her hand on the door, she smiled at him. "Are you ready?"

"As much as I'll ever be," he said, not sounding too sure of himself.

Inside, the table was set for four; the food was already laid out. Emma's mother stood at the stove, her back to them. Her father stood waiting, dressed in his Sunday best.

Emma stood between her father and Anthony, to make the introductions. It was all done very proper. "Papa, this is Anthony Watson."

"It's a pleasure to meet you, sir," Anthony said, offering his hand.

The two shook hands. It was an unspoken contest of strength. Simon's grip was like a vise, getting stronger every moment, not letting go. Anthony's first impulse was to tighten his grip and let the man taste some of his own medicine. Then he thought of what Emma told him. He decided to grin and bear it, which in its own way put him in good light. He proved himself man enough to stand up to a situation.

"You're Edna and Armand Watson's boy, ain't you?" Simon asked. Clearly a question he knew the answer to, and everyone else knew he did. Still, it broke the ice and set the mood.

"Sit down, sit down," Simon told Anthony, gesturing to a chair at the table, sounding overly gracious and formal.

Anthony had the good sense not to sit till Simon and Emma took their seat. Cora was still at the stove, Anthony stood waiting.

"Sit down, son. If you're waitin' on Cora, you'll have a time of it. She ain't much for sittin' when she's cookin'. She'll sit in her own time."

"Thank you, sir," Antony said, taking a seat. He wasn't sure if the room was warm, but he was beginning to sweat.

"So, how old are you now, son?"

"Seventeen, sir, but not for long, I'll be eighteen next month.

"You father any babies?"

"Papa…?" shouted Emma in embarrassment.

"What…?" Simon said with surprise. "All of us know what life on a plantation can be like. I want to know if he's got any children."

"No, sir, I've never been with a woman."

"Well, I don't think I'd be braggin' on that, but it's a good thing to know. I got more to ask you, but I'll wait till my wife joins us. Cora, are you about ready?"

The sound of pots and pans clanging was his answer. All air of friendliness, left the room,

Without a word, Cora came to the table, placing down a bowl of greens. She took a seat opposite Emma,

"Nice to meet you, Mrs. Tucker," Anthony said, smiling.

Cora just gave him a nod. Her face was blank. Anthony couldn't read into, although Emma and Simon recognized it immediately. It was the look of disinterest mixed with annoyance and just a twinge of anger.

"Going to be eighteen, are you? That's a great age to be," Simon said in hopes of dispersing the dark cloud that hung over the table. It helped for a moment, and then that moment was gone.

Simon continued, "So, Anthony, tell us about yourself."

"Well, sir, my parents raised me right. I'm churchgoer, as you know." He stopped for a moment, took in a deep breath, and closed his eyes. "And I'm in love with your daughter, sir."

"That's what I hear, son."

"And I'd like to marry her, sir," Anthony finished, opening to see what damage he might have caused.

"Are you askin' for my daughter's hand in marriage?" Simon asked.

Anthony's first thought was to say, *isn't that what I just said?* However, he thought before he spoke. He realized telling a father you want to married marry his daughter is not the same as asking for her hand. The man just wanted to be shown respect. A slave is so often treated with disrespect, most of their life, respect is cherished. Simon was known as a good man, and worthy of his moment.

"Yes, sir, I'm asking you for your daughter's hand in marriage." There, he said it proper.

Simon was smiling. "Well, I guess we can talk about it."

"Don't I have a say in all this?" Cora said, staring forward, not looking at anyone, directly. "She my daughter, too, you know?"

"Of course, Cora, of course," Simon told her in his softest voice. "What is it you want to say?"

"Why are you in such a hurry to give our daughter away to someone we don't even know?"

"I only said we'd talk about it," Simon replied. He thought it over, his mind was racing. He wanted to make everyone happy, starting with his wife. "I think I have a solution," he said. "Let's look at a long engagement."

This announcement had the opposite affect he'd hoped for. It did not go well with the others. Emma and Anthony looked disappointed, to say the least. Their faces became long and drawn, as they stared at him in confusion, whereas, Cora looked perturbed with more than a hint of annoyance and a woman's fury.

"How long of an engagement were you thinking?" Emma asked, nearly in tears as she looked to her father, then to Antony, and then back to her father.

No one dared look at Cora.

"Oh, I don't know," Simon replied. "How does a year sound?"

Again, this announcement did not sit well with the others.

"Papa…!" Emma sounded.

"All right…how about six months?" he said, trying his best to find a compromise. There was a slight pleading in his voice. "That's it, I've made my decision. There will be a six-month engagement!" he announced.

Once again, none of them showed enthusiasm. It was clear to all that Cora did not like any of it. Simon dreaded when he and his wife were alone. He knew she had something on her mind, and that she was sure to give him a piece of it. Nevertheless, Simon would have the last word. He put his foot down and trudge on.

Both Emma and Anthony, though clearly disappointed, were willing to accept the father's wishes. They let out a sigh of relief. After all, they had cleared the first hurtle. A six-month engagement or not, they had gotten Simon's blessing. Finally, they could go to Reverend, and set a date for the wedding.

"Oh, and by the way," Simon directed his words to Anthony. "I think we should set up a meeting with your parent."

"Yes, sir, I'll try to make that happen."

Pleased with himself, Simon was the only one with a look of content.

****

Thankfully, the meeting of the Tucker and Watson families was better than Emma and Anthony expected.

Why the two families had not been on better terms over the years was a mystery. They were slaves of the same master, worked the same fields, and attended the same church. Still, there was a distance be the two families. Not imposed by anyone, but a distance, nonetheless.

It was an evening dinner of the two families at the Watson home. Edna pulled out all the stops, cooking all her signature dishes. Armand even acquired a bottle of sipping whiskey, and a plug of good chewing tobacco. The Watson's were determined to putting their best foot forward.

Everyone one, the Tuckers and the Watsons, interacted, as if they'd known one another for years, which in a sense they had, only from afar. There were even moments of good conversation, and above all laughter. They had more in common that not, immediately mingling as if one family.

The two fathers, Armand and Simon hit it off well, telling stories, slapping each other on the back at the end of each tale. Perhaps, drinking a bit more whiskey then they should have, but it a special occasion.

The mothers were the same, carrying on like two long-lost sisters. Everyone agreed they all had so much in common; it was a shame they remained distant from one another for so many years.

Emma and Anthony smiled at each other with relief. Six months would be a long time waiting to marry. Still, it would be six months without turmoil.

It was all going so well. That was why none of them noticed the meeting of the two mothers at the stove, done in whispers.

"We need to meet," Edna said to Cora.

"I know…I know," Cora agreed, "When and where?"

"Make an excuse to go to the church on Wednesday night. The choir rehearses between six and seven. Meet me at the church a little after seven."

Four

Meeting at the Church

Cora hid behind a tree, waiting for the choir to leave the church. When they left, she entered, finding Edna, alone, standing before the pulpit. As she approached, their eyes met. The pain in their faces increased, till they stood a few feet from each other. Without a word spoken, they both burst into tears. Edna reached out; they fell into each other's arms, sobbing.

It was a minute before they regained themselves. Hand in hand, they sat in the first pew, face-to-face.

"What are we going to do?" Cora cried.

The question echoed around them, it weighed upon them like a great heaviness, stifling their breath, their thoughts, their lives.

Cora continued. "We can't let this happen, Edna."

Edna's lower lip quivered as she spoke, "We need to tell them."

"There must be another way?" Cora asked.

"There is no other way," Edna continued. "I wish there was another way, but I can't for the life of me think of it."

"It will kill them," Cora replied. "Then they will know, and so will everyone else, even our husband. I never thought this would happen."

"I know…I know," Edna agreed.

They both fell silent, lost in thought.

"We need to tell them soon, before they do something foolish," Edna added.

"My daughter is not like that; she would never do anything before getting married."

"Cora, they're young. Don't you remember what it was like? I know my son, he's a good boy, but a young man can only behave for so long."

There was another long silence.

"We don't have to say anything. What if we just kept it to ourselves?" Cora asked.

"Cora, you want to take that chance. What happens when they try to have children?"

"Maybe, nothing will happen."

"I said children, Cora, not child. So what if the first child is fine? What about the second or third child? You want to keep worrying for the rest of you like? Besides, it's not fair to them, or us. If they ever learn the truth, knowing we knew all along, they will never speak to us again. Neither will our husbands."

"I'm just so scared, Edna. I say we take the chance. What they don't know won't hurt them."

"God will know..." said a voice from the back of the church. They spun around to see Pastor Jefferies walking toward them.

For what reason, they felt uncomfortable with a common shame, unable to look him directly in the eye, as he stood before them.

"I believe I understand what you two have been discussing, but I want hear it from you." They remained silent. "Perhaps, I can help. It is my job, you know."

They looked up to him, shyly. Cora turned to Edna, a forlorn look in her eyes. Edna knew what that look meant. Cora was pleading with her to speak for them both. Slowly and softly, Edna made a beginning.

"As you know, Cora and I are about the same age; we both married at the same time." Edna stopped, the words caught in her throat, tears running down her cheeks. Jefferies found a chair, pulled it in close, and sat down.

"It's all right, Edna...it's all right," he said tenderly.

Cora reached over to Edna, the two desperately held onto each other.

Thinking there was no easy way to say what needed saying; Edna came straight out with it. "Anthony and Emma are brother and sister."

Even though he expected as much, a look of shock washed over Jefferies' face.

"There I've said it. Cora and I were both raped by the same man. He is the true father of our children."

It took all his strength to ask, fear taking hold of him. "Who is the father?"

Edna lifted her watery eyes, looking into his. "Massa Malum..."

"He raped us both, like he's done to so other many women, here," Cora added, herself in tears.

Jefferies was beyond stunned. "This is the first I've ever heard of this," he said, almost demanding an answer.

"Well, how many women do you think want to be found out, folks pointing there fingers at you? Not to mention what it would do to their marriages. One in ten of the children on this plantation were fathered by Malum."

"Then both your husbands believe they are the fathers of your children?"

Cora nodded. "We never thought something like this would happen. Edna and I did all we could. We were friends when we were little girls. When this happened, we stayed away from each other, afraid of what might happen. I've prayed so hard for so many years, and this is God's answer?"

Jefferies let out a long sigh, as he shook his head. "We have to do something." They all knew it was just talk, wishful thinking. Their choices were limited. He rose from his chair. "There's no way around it. You two will have to tell your children who their real father is."

They looked up at him, as if he were a judge who just past a death sentence on both of them.

"He's right," Cora announced. "They deserve the truth. The decision is up to them. They need to know."

There was nothing left to be said. The women stood, brushing themselves.

"When should we do it?" Edna asked Cora.

"As soon as possible," Jefferies interjected. "You can bring your families here to the church, if you need a somewhere. If you want, I will be a part of it. I will help however I can."

"That would be good, Reverend," Edna responded. "When would be a good time/"

"Would Saturday night work?"

"We'll bring our families, then," Cora answered.

The two women walked up arm in arm, toward the door.

"Oh, and Cora," Reverend Jefferies call out "In the beginning, God gave us a perfect world. It's now a fallen world. We're the one who made it this way. Don't go blaming God for what we did. But don't go blaming yourselves, either. You two women are innocent of all wrongdoing."

"Tell that to our husband," Edna replied.

"Thank you again, Reverend Jefferies," Cora called back from the door.

"I will be praying for y'all," he concluded.

"Thanks, we'll need it," Edna said as they left the church.

Outside, the women walked slowly, silently, arm in arm toward the slave quarters.

"How do you think they'll react?" Cora asked.

"Like we've offered them poison. They'll never trust us again."

"Who…the children or our husbands…?"

"All of them," Edna replied.

"Do you think they'll stay together, Emma and Anthony?"

"I don't know, stay together, break apart, it all seems so hopeless."

"How will your husband take it?" Cora asked.

"He'll probably kill me."

A chill flew up Cora's spin. She knew Edna wasn't' just throwing out a jest to make clever conversation, Armand might truly try to kill her. She thought of her husband, Simon. "I hurt Simon in the past, but nothing like this. I don't want to loose him, Edna. We've been together so long; I don't want to throw it all away. I love him so much!"

Edna had no answer, she nodded her head knowingly.

At the slave quarters, they hugged and kissed good-bye. Nothing was said, just two women in the moonlight, turning toward their homes, walking away from each other.

Cora told her husband not to expect her till late. She was going to the church to listen to the choir. She was thinking of joining.

She tiptoed in the dark, not to wake her daughter or husband. When she got in bed, Simon stirred slightly.

"You think you might join the church choir?" he asked never opening his eyes, his voice floating around the dark room like a mist.

"No, I don't think so."

"Why not, you've got a good voice?"

"I just don't' feel like singing, lately."

****

The next day, working in the fields, both Edna and Cora took notice of Emma and Anthony working side by side. What they saw made them worry all the more, wondering if Saturday night was not soon enough.

Every so often, the couple would look at each other and smile. This was nothing unusual for a young couple in love. Only, knowing their true relation to each other stuck a warning into the veins of both women.

But what was more concerning was the moment after the smile. That moment when the young couple looked into each other's eyes with a longing that cannot be described, both mothers understood. It was only natural that two young people in love yearn for each other. Within the confines of marriage, it is encouraged. It is how the human race perpetuates, through time, generation after generation.

For Edna and Cora, dreading the confrontation about to happen, Saturday couldn't come soon enough.

"Are you sure about what you're doing?" Cora asked Emma, as they both stood in the field, looking at Anthony working off in the distance.

"How did you know Papa was the one for you?" Emma asked, never taking her eyes off Anthony.

"Oh, I don't know. It was more of a feeling that anything else. I just sort of knew."

"I'd say it's the same way with Anthony and me."

"But how does he make you feel? Does he make you happy?"

Emma smiled and chuckle a little. "You know I've never thought about it, my happiness, that is. I always seem more concerned with his happiness. I guess you could say that making him happy makes me happy."

Cora watched her daughter walk away, starry-eyed.

Later in the day, standing next to her, Cora whispered to Edna.

"We need to do whatever we can to keep them separated."

Cora didn't need to explain, Edna knew what she meant.

"Why, do you think they've done it?" Edna asked.

"If they hadn't, they will," Cora answered.

Then Edna voiced the fear that haunted them both. "What if we tell them, and they still continue?"

It was a possibility neither one wanted to face. Cora didn't answer. She sighted, bowed her head, working her way across the field, away from Edna.

Five

Tell Me It Doesn't Matter

Saturday took forever to come, and it came so quickly. All concerned gathered at the church. Edna and Cora were not met with protest from the others, only with questions, which they wouldn't answer, not until the meeting. They all suspected, since the meeting was at the church and Reverend Jefferies was in attendance, it was to talk about the wedding.

At the front of the church, in front of the pews, Jefferies arrange chairs in a circle. Everyone took a seat, facing one another.

"Will someone finally tell me why we're here?" Armand grumbled, looking from face to face.

"It's about Emma and Anthony," Jefferies announced. The young couple smiled, believing only the best was coming.

"Edna...Cora, would either one of you like to start us off," Jefferies asked the two women.

Edna and Cora stared at each other, waiting and hoping the other would speak. Finally, Edna took the initiative. Looking directly at Emma and Anthony, leaning forward, she spoke softly.

"Life's not always what we think. It doesn't always give you what you want. Sometimes it can be unfair." She halted for a long moment.

"For heaven sake, Edna, what the hell are you trying to say!" Armand shouted at his wife.

Edna was speechless. She looked to Cora for help, only to find none. Then, she looked with sorrowful eyes to her pastor.

"Would you like me to continue?" Jefferies asked. No one spoke. The sad looks on Edna's and Cora's face gave him permission. All eyes were on him. Except, his words were addressed mostly to Emma and Anthony.

"I'm going to talk two you both like adults. I want you to act like adults." He looked to the husbands. "Armand...Simon, I want you both to do the same and stay calm." Everyone sat up straight and wide-eyed. He couldn't have gotten their attention any better if he'd pointed a pistol at them. He returned his gaze back to Emma and Anthony.

"There's not easy way to say this, so I'm just going to come right out and say it. Edna and Cora are your mothers, but I'm afraid these men are not your fathers."

"What the hell do you mean by that?" Armand shouted, jumping to his feet.

"Armand...please," Jefferies pleaded, gesturing for Armand to sit, again. "Please, Armand, let me explain. Armand took his seat reluctantly. Jefferies continued, "Both your mothers were raped." He hesitated for a moment, and then he added, "By the same man."

Armand jumped up again. This time he shouted at his wife, "Is this true?"

Edna lowered her eyes to the floor and nodded.

Still staring down at Edna, Armand pointed at Anthony. "Are you saying that Anthony is not really my son?"

Still staring at the floor, Edna nodded, again.

Simon couldn't speak. He looked to Cora with sorrowful eyes. Like Edna, she couldn't look her husband in the eyes. She nodded before the question was asked.

"Then who is the father?" Armand shouted.

"Massa Malum," Edna said in a whisper.

"He fathered both these children?" Simon asked as calmly as he could. "Cora, look at me. I want to hear it from you and you alone. Is Massa Malum the father of these two children?"

Cora looked up, her cheeks washed with tears. "Yes..."

Anthony spoke up. The statement wasn't directed at any person in particular, just anyone who could answer his question, even God. "Does that mean Emma and me are brother and sister?"

"Only half brother and sister," Reverend Jefferies added, as if the words *only* and *half* would soften the blow.

Anthony sprang from his seat, facing Emma; he took her arms and lifted her up. She was beside herself, in tears.

"Tell me, it doesn't matter," he said softly, at first. She was crying profusely. Tears covered her entire face. She rocked her head from side to side, trying desperately not to look him in the eyes. "Tell me, it doesn't matter," he repeated.

She was unable to answer, shaking in his grasp.

"I love you, Emma," he shouted.

"I love you, too," she said, collapsing into near-unconsciousness.

"I love you," he kept repeating, unable to get her to respond. "Tell me, it doesn't matter."

She fell down onto her chair. She rested her head in her hands. Still, crying.

"This is a lie; it's got to be," Anthony demanded. "Emma…Emma."

She was unable to respond, her tearful eyes looking up at him.

Anthony tilted his head back, shouting to heaven, "No…!"

No one said a word. Suddenly, a look came over Anthony, a look of desperation, anger, and worst of all…madness.

They all watched in amazement as he leaped onto the first pew. Running the full length of the pew, when he got to the end, he jumped, crashing through the oversized window. Shards of glass flew in every direction. Jefferies ran to the window He could see Anthony running toward the woods. A moment later he was gone.

Cora rushed to her daughter, the others standing behind her.

"Are you all right, baby?" Cora asked, holding Emma up in the chair.

Emma stirred, still dazed, a cold distant look in her eyes.

"Everyone, listen to me," Pastor Jefferies called out. "This has been a difficult day. Y'all need to go to your homes and heal. Try to understand, forgive, but most of all heal. What has happened does not change anything. You were a family before you came here today, y'all are still a family. Remember the love, because that never changes."

Jefferies wasn't sure any of them even heard him. They looked in shock, as they stood up.

Slowly, they starting for the door. Each of them would have to deal with their pain in their own way. Cora and Simon guided Emma along. Armand was first to leave, clearly upset, leaving Edna behind. Edna stood on the church steps looking out at the woods, knowing her son was out there, hurt, and there was nothing she could do about it.

****

Anthony never returned home that night. The next day, when he was not in the fields working, he was reported as missing. Overseer, Monk, made his account directly to Fergus Malum.

"Mr. Malum, it seems we've got a rabbit on the run," Monk accounted.

"Which one…?" Fergus asked.

"Anthony Watson, a youngin', late teens," replied Monk.

Fergus let out a sigh of disgust. "Take three men with you, track him down. He can't be far off. When you find him, bring him back."

The reason for this last statement was because Fergus believed that when an example is made, it sends fear throughout the slave community. Fear is power. In his mind,

Anthony was a dead man. To kill him right out would be a waste, best to have him suffer and die slowly in front of the entire plantation.

It's important to note here that Fergus Malum held no idea that Anthony was his son. He had no though about how many of his slaves were actually his offspring. Obviously, some of the children born to these women must be his. He knew that. He raped as many slave women as he wanted, as often as he wanted, over the years. Children were of no consequence to him.

Fergus' wife, Estella, suspected her husband of wild infidelities. She understood this to be his prerogative. Still, she didn't like it. She knew of other wives of plantation owners that were not bothered by their husbands black mistresses; some even approved and endorsed the action. Estella found it best to ignore it, turn her head, and make believe it never happens. Nevertheless, it chafed her to no end. If an opportunity appeared when she not only could stop her husband, but even punish him for his behavior, she would take it. As unlikely as that opportunity seemed, she silently hoped for it.

Six

Hope and Punishment

Two days later, in the evening, the Tucker family ate supper in silence. Emma was clearly better, although not well. No one spoke, for what was there to say? The fear was anything said would only make matters worse.

Unable to eat, Emma stood, walking to the door.

"Are you all right, dear?" Cora asked.

"I'm just fine. I need to be alone, if you don't mind."

When it was obvious none of them were interested in eating, Cora began to clear the table. Finally, Simon voiced what was on his mind.

"You know you hurt me, Cora," he said in a gentle tone, sounding like a small boy who'd bruised his knee.

"I know…I'm sorry. But it wasn't my fault."

"What wasn't you're fault?" he asked. "Of course, it was your fault."

"Simon, I was raped. It wasn't my fault."

"That's not what I'm talking about, Cora. I know all that. No one could blame you for that. You were a victim. What I'm talking about you hiding it from me. I'm your husband, Cora. It's in the marriage vows – respect, isn't it? That's what you owed me – respect. You could have come to me with anything. You supposed to come to me. It would have been hard, but we would have found a way. Instead, you hid from me like I was a stranger. When have I ever purposely tried to hurt you? It would have been difficult, but we would have got through it. And what about Emma, she deserves more, too."

Even though he felt a need to get all this off his chest, just by looking at her he realized his words were cutting deep into her. He stopped immediately.

"I love you, Cora."

"I love you, too, Simon."

"Then don't ever hide anything from me, again. What's mine is yours and what's yours is mine. We can see our way through it."

"I'm sorry, will you ever forgive me?"

"I already have, only, please, trust me."

"I will. I promise. I love you, Simon."

"I love you, too," he said, again, walking toward the door.

"Where are you going?"

"I need to check on Emma."

Cora continued to clear the table.

Outside, Simon found Emma on the porch, standing, staring into the darkness.

"Are you all right?" he asked.

Emma looked back over her shoulder, smiling at him. "Yes…no…I mean…" Her thought scattered. "I'm fine, Papa," she said, touched by his concern, not wanting to burden him with any of the weight that was on her heart.

He moved next to her, helping her stare down the night.

"You know, Emma, after what we've learned today, you don't have to call me Papa, anymore."

She took his hand, and turned to him. "I've only know one father. You have been there all my life. You were my father, you are my father, and you will always be my father."

A tear rolled down the side of his cheek. He leaned over and kissed her.

"Have you decided what you're going to do?" he asked. They both knew what he meant.

"No, I don't," she replied. "I'm confused, Papa. So much has changed, yet so much remains the same. I still love him, Papa. I can't stop. I've tried, I've prayed, but I can't stop loving Anthony."

"And you shouldn't," Simon said softly. "There nothing in this world like love. Once it comes, it can go, but it can never die."

Emma continued to look intently the night's nothingness before them.

"You know, he's not going to just appear."

"Not tonight, maybe, but he will someday," Emma announced with confidence.

Simon kissed her cheek once, turned, and entered the house.

"Is Emma all right?" Cora asked him.

"No, not yet, but she will be."

****

Monk and his men returned empty-handed. Fergus was not one to give up so easily. He ordered Monk to gather a week's worth of supplies and try again to find Anthony. However, before he could do so, there were other problems on the plantation that needed looking after.

That morning, after the headcount, they were two workers short, besides Anthony. It didn't take long to realize the missing slaves were Edna and Armand Wilson. Monk took aside Little George, a twelve-year-old lad, the fastest runner on the plantation.

"I want ya to run down to the slave quarters. Ya tell Edna and Armand Wilson if they don't get their butts to work real soon, I'm gonna have their hides ripped off of `em. Ya understand?"

Little George nodded and ran off. No less than three minutes later, the lad retuned. He was sweating and out of breath from the run.

"So, where are they?" Monk asked.

Little George stood silent, his eyes wide with fear.

"I asked ya a question, boy!" Monk shouted.

Still, there was no response from Little George. The shouting only made it worse. Little George began shaking with panic.

Monk gave the lad the back of his hand, hard. Little George flew backwards, falling to the floor.

"Idiot," Monk barked as he walked off toward the slave quarters. *If ya want anything done right…* he grumbled aloud to himself

Monk was angry. It showed in his face and by the way he swaggered up to the shack. Standing on the porch of the Watson home, he wasn't about to dignify them with a knock. He kicked in the door, and entered the one-room shack. The windows were covered. Only the light pouring through the doorway entered. A shaft of light landed on Armand, sitting motionless in a chair.

"Armand, what the hell ya think ya doin'? Monk shouted as he entered. A few feet in, he stopped. What he saw sent a chill though him, from head to toe.

Sprawled out of the floor, at Armand's feet, was a lifeless Edna, her throat cut from ear to ear. Her eyes were open, none blinking. Her body twisted in an unnatural position. Surprisingly, there was little blood. Most of it drained through the crack of the wooden floor. It was a horrible sight.

"What the hell have ya done?" Monk said, taking his gun from his holster. His aim shook, as he pointed the gun at Armand. "Stand up, Armand," Monk ordered.

Armand smiled a madman's smile, as he rose from his seat, which frightened Monk all the more.

"She was a good woman," Armand said softly, still smiling. "I loved her. But a man can only take so much."

Monk had no idea what Armand meant, nor did he care. "Get along, Armand," Monk ordered, waving his pistol at the door. Without a word or a fuse, Armand silently did as he was told. Monk kept his aim on Armand as they left the shack.

Standing in the sunlight, Armand covered his eyes from the brightness. "I did love her, you know?"

****

For five days, they kept Armand in a metal cage, outside the main house. Actually, it was once a rabbit hutch. The white and dark splotches of rabbit dung were still on the floor of the cage. Guards were placed on constant watch to prevent anyone from helping him to escape.

Everyday before working in the fields, the slaves were marched past the cage. No one was allowed to look down or away. Each day Armand looked worse, till on the six day, he looked like he'd die any minute.

"If you're going to kill him, then let me kill him," Fergus's son, Douglas, said laughingly. "What are you waiting for?" he asked, not understanding his father's logic.

Fergus sighed, shaking his head, yet he was glad in knowing it would be a learning moment for his son.

"You're still a young man, Douglas. Young men can afford to vivacious and careless. One day this plantation will be all yours. If you're ever going to run it like a man, you need to understand something. Fear is the only thing these people understand. You must instill it in them, everyday, and every change you get, as deeply as you can. Never waste an opportunity to send them a message of terror."

Douglas took his father's advice to heart, as if it were Gospel. It was like a light shone down from heaven to bestow enlightenment to him. He knew his was to be relentless in his beliefs.

"We're going to execute that slave, today. You will be there at my side to witness it."

"It would be a honor, father."

A pride like no other filled Fergus. At that moment, if he had been the type of man who exhibits his emotions, he would have showed it.

****

The sunrise was in full bloom over the world when they gathered all the slaves and workers in front of the main house. Fergus stood on the porch, watching with his son at his side.

34

They pulled Armand from his cage. He could barely stand, let alone walk. He'd lost much weight. His eyes sank deep into his skull. There was only a few more hours of life left in him.

The overseers dragged Armand to a post anchored in the ground. They Armand against the post, wrapping a link chain around him to hold him in place. Then they placed sticks and logs at his feet, dowsing the wood with kerosene.

"I want you all to pay close attention. This could happen to you. There will be no mercy for disobedience. Everyone, pay attention…everyone!" As he spoke these words, Fergus turned his head to his son. "Everyone!" he repeated.

To add to the effect, Monk lit a torch. The flame was large, for all to see. He slowly brought the torch to the pile of wood. Everyone could smell the kerosene. It would go aflame in the flicker of an eye.

Just as he was about to touch the touch to the firewood, a rifle shot rang out from off in the distance. The bullet hit Armand between the eyes. His head went flying back; blood spurted like a small geyser. He went stiff for a second, and then limp, the chain holding him up. His head fell forward, the blood falling on the wood at his feet.

"Mr. Malum…?" Monk shouted, not sure of what to do.

"The shot came from the west. Take some of your men, saddle up, and catch whoever did this."

"Yes, sir…!" Monk replied. "I need you, you, and you," he said, pointing to three of his men. "Ya heard Mr. Malum…saddle up!" He dropped the torch to the ground, and was about to follow his men to the barn when Fergus called to him.

"Have you forgotten something?"

"What, sir…" Monk called back.

"The punishment, you were about to deliver."

"But he's already dead, sir."

"I don't care. That's not the point. A punishment was called for!"

"Yes, sir…" Monk said, shrugging his shoulders. It made no sense to him. Still the boss is law. He hesitantly picking up the torch, and then igniting the wood at the dead man's feet.

The twigs caught first and fast, then the sticks, and then the logs. The flames licked over Armand's body. Everyone watched in horror. His clothing went up in a blaze, then his body and hair. His entire body was an inferno. It was a strange sight to see, a person on fire, not moving a muscle.

"May I leave now?" Doulas asked his father, sounding board.

"Go on, it's enough for one day," Fergus surmised.

Everyone turned when the sound of Monk and the others rode off into the west in pursuit of the shooter.

"Eyes where they belong!" Fergus shouted.

They stood there for a full hour, until he dismissed them. The flames ate up the flesh down to the bone. The body fell to the ground, indistinguishable to the burning logs. The chain remained wrapped around the post, glowing red hot.

Seven

The Man Who Owned the World

All was quiet. The slaves were working in the fields. Monk and his men were still wandering the forest, looking for Anthony and the shooter of Armand, whom they suspected as being one and the same.

As he'd done many times before, Douglas accompanied his mother into town, for a day of shopping.

Fergus was alone in the main house. Left to his own devises, he could only think of his two main vices: drunkenness and philandering. Understandably, they usually walked hand in hand, starting with the first and then the later.

Fergus found Little George in the kitchen, scrubbing the floor.

"Stop what you're doing. I want you to run an errand for me."

Little George dropped the brush in the bucket, stood up straight as a soldier , giving his full attention.

"Go to the fields. I want you to fetch Phyllis for me."

"She the one who's about so high," Little George said, holding his hand at his chin. "She the one with the chipped tooth in front?"

"That's right. Go to the fields and fetch her back to me. I'll be in the parlor, you bring her there."

"Yes, sir," Little George said, rushing out the kitchen door.

Waiting in the parlor, Fergus prepared. He'd anticipated this day for weeks. It would be a special occasion, only the best would do. He took down his oldest and most expensive bottle of bourbon, poured himself a tall glass, and began to drink. Not sipping, mind you, but full gulps. By the time Little George returned with Phyllis, Fergus was on his third glass, and his head was swimming.

"You can go, now," Fergus ordered the boy. "Close the door behind you."

Little George did as he was told. Before closing the door, he looked to Phyllis. Even at his young age, he knew something was amiss. He couldn't catch her eye. The poor girl stood, frightened, staring at the floor. When the door closed, she flinched at the sound.

Fergus walked to the door and locked, he didn't want anyone walking in, unexpectedly. Nor did he want anyone to leave.

Phyllis was petite, a girl of fourteen, with just a whisper of womanhood blossoming within her. She was known for her shyness, like a small woodland creature, her sad eyes, always on the verge of tears, and her chipped front tooth.

Standing before her, with a full glass of bourbon, he snapped at her, "Look at me, girl." When she continued to stare timidly at the floor, he took hold of her chin, pushing it upwards.

Slowly, she raised her head.

"That's better," he said. "Now, listen to me. We can do this one of two ways. You can do everything I tell you to do, and when you leave I will see that your life is better for it. Or you can disobey me, in which case, I will force myself upon you, and I'll still get what I want. You can leave this room alive, or I'll have them carry your dead body out of her. So, what's it going to be?"

Phyllis remained silent.

"So be it," Fergus proclaimed, slugging down his whiskey, tossing the glass across the room. The sound of glass shattering forced Phyllis to recoil from him. He pulled her in close, pressing his lips to hers. She moaned sorrowful, wriggling to free herself from his grasp. He was too strong for her, it was useless.

Her discomfort only excited him, all the more. She pulled back with all her might. In frustration, he gave her the back of his hand, slamming her to the floor.

He took hold of her arms, lifter her to her feet, and tossed her aside. She landed on the divan. The next instant he was on top of her. His hands groping her, she twisted frantically, trying to break free. He tore at her blouse till she was exposed to him. Bringing his head back, he began kissing her flesh. All the while, Phyllis cried and pleaded in his ear. Only it was too late, he was deafened by lust.

Suddenly, Fergus felt the hard press of steel against the back of his head. He stopped moving, waiting and listening. Then he heard it – the sound of metal clicking against metal. He recognized the familiar resonance immediately. It was the hammer of a rifle locking back into place.

"Get off her," a voice demanded. Fergus raised his hands in submission. He slowly raised himself off Phyllis. "Now!" shouted the voice. Fergus rushed to his feet in compliance.

Standing up, his hands still raised, Fergus recognized his assailant. It was Anthony, pointing a rifle at Fergus' gut.

"You…" Fergus remarked in surprise.

"Yes…me."

Fergus glance over at the door. It was still closed and locked. He looked about the room. How had he entered? Curtains fluttered. There was an open window.

Phyllis sat up, trying to make sense of her shredded blouse to cover herself. She held the strips of material across her breasts.

"Go home," Anthony said softly.

At first, Phyllis was too confused to move.

"Go home," he repeated.

This time the message found its mark. Phyllis ran from the room, not looking back. She tried to open the door. When it wouldn't open, she became frantic. She fumbled with the lock on the door. When she got it open, she flew out of the room, down the hall, and out the front door.

"My men are out looking for you," Fergus said in anger.

"Well, they didn't find me," Anthony answered sarcastically. "You can put your hands down, now."

Fergus lowered his hands, "Why haven't you killed me, already?"

"Who says I'm going to kill you? I may and then might not."

Fergus looked into Anthony's eyes, trying to decipher his chances. Nothing came back to him, except a blank, cold stare.

Anthony continued, "I want to tell you a story. Once upon a time, there was a man who owned the world. I mean it; he owned the entire world, all the land and everything on it, including the people. Now, he didn't rule the people, not like a king. He set himself like a god over his people. He forced them to work for him, never giving them anything in return, not even their own lives. He gave them nothing but suffering.

"Until one day the people said they'd have no more of him. They rebelled, refusing to bow down, to worship him, to never obey him again. And you know what they did next?"

"They killed him," Fergus replies, half answer, half question.

"No, no, they would never do that. Death would be too good for him. You must understand that he made these people suffer, not only for all their own lives, but for generations of lives, before and after them. Death would only erase him; it would not be equal to their suffering. So you know what they did? They let him live, and live a long time, too. Only, it would be a life of torment. A life that would make the story of Job look like a cakewalk. Years of tears, taking away everything that was his until there was nothing or nobody left in his life. Till he begged for death, yet he lived on." Anthony looked for Fergus' reaction. There was none. "So, what do you think of my story?"

"You won't get away with this," was Fergus' reaction.

"Oh, there's more to the story," Anthony continued. "This man, who owned the world, used the women for his own pleasure. He fathered many children, yet he didn't care for them. He didn't even acknowledge their existence."

"Oh, now I understand," Fergus said. "You're one of those. What are you the black sheep of the family, the prodigal son demanding his fair inheritance? Well, let me tell you, boy. You're right I do own the world, and your part of my world. I own you, and I always will. To me you're nothing but livestock. And you, you're nothing but a half-breed, a mistake of nature. If you're going to kill me, you better do it now. Because if you don't, I will hunt you down, and when I do, you'll regret you didn't."

Anthony just smiled, slowly backing toward the door. "No, I'll take my chances. I'll live to see you suffer."

"And how do you intend to do that?" Fergus asked.

"By taking away your life, piece by piece, everything you hold dear will slip through you fingers like sand. And the harder you grasp, the more sand will slip away."

Fergus exploded into laughter. "You think you'll win? Two can play that game."

Anthony shot an inquisitive look a Fergus. "What do you mean?"

"You stupid boy, you have more of your mother in you than your father, obviously. I have far more power than you could ever imagine. Every time you come down on me, I will come crashing down on you like an avalanche. If you hurt anyone I love, I will do the same. Do you understand me?"

"Then it's all-out war?"

"If that's what you what you want to call it, then yes, it's all-out war. You've bitten off more than you can chew, boy."

At that moment, the doors flew open. Unaware, Monk came rushing in. "Mr. Malum, I..."

Anthony quickly spun around, pointing his rifle at him. Monk stopped midsentence, standing still, raising his hands up.

"What were you just about to say?" Anthony asked.

Monk looked to Fergus for a sign.

"It's all right, Monk. Let's hear what you were about to say."

"I was going to say that we weren't able to find the shooter," he said, with a tone of uncomfortable shame.

Anthony just laughed, circling slowly around Monk, making his way out of the room.

Standing in the doorway, he looked one last time at Fergus. "Till we meet again, father..."

"Go to hell, my son."

Eight

It's Gonna Be All Right

The sun hung high in the sky, moving in its slow journey to the west. The heat was intense. The overseers allowed more water brakes for the workers. Not out of compassion, only necessity. If the crop was to be brought in, it would take all hands.

Cora worked alongside her husband and daughter. Simon was a good worker, always concentrating on the task before him, which is why he didn't notice. It was Cora who realized something was wrong. She turned to see Emma, hunched over and motionless.

"Sweetheart, what's the matter?" Cora asked.

Emma didn't answer.

Cora looked to her husband, "Simon, there's something wrong with Emma."

Simon rushed to his daughter's side. "Emma, are you all right?"

Still, she gave no answer.

"What's goin' on here?" one of the overseers asked, walking toward them, his rifle under his arm.

The next instant, Emma collapsed face down in the dirt.

"She's sick, she needs help," Cora demanded.

"All right," said the overseer. "Take her back home." He addressed this statement to Simon, alone.

Simon lifted Emma up in his arms, carrying her off. He looked back one last time to see Cora standing, watching, and feeling helpless and worried.

"You, you get back to work," the overseer told Cora.

Emma moaned in his arms. "Don't worry, baby, we'll be home soon," Simon whispered.

In their home, he laid her down on her bed. He offered her a cup of water. He couldn't get her to drink. His hand upon her forehead told him she had a fever. Unable to help, Simon ran out of the shack and across the compound.

"Who is it?" a frail woman's voice seeped through the door.

"Simon Tucker, ma'am…"

"What do ya want?"

"It's my daughter, she's not well."

"What's that to me?"

"Please, we need your help."

It was well known throughout the plantation; Harriet Langley knew the old ways, ointments and potions from herbs, flowers, barks, and all sorts of growth in the forest and fields. Some believed she was a witch. Still, this never stopped them from seeking her help when someone was ill.

He heard the sound of creaking wood as she walked across the room. The door opened slowly with an ear piercing squeal.

Harriet Langley was the oldest slave on the plantation, perhaps in the entire county. Now, too old to work the fields, she always kept to herself, usually in her home. Simon hadn't seen her in three years. She looked exactly as he remembered her. A thin, frail little woman, she came up to Simon's chest.

"Take me to her," Harriet said, sounding imposed on.

In his worry, Simon wanted them to move faster. Harriet moved too slowly for his liking.

"Quit hovering over me like a vulture," the old woman complained.

"Sorry," Simon said, not wanting to get on her bad side.

Entering the shack, Harriet went straight to Emma's bedside.

"Go wait outside,' she ordered Simon.

"Is there anything you need?" Simon asked.

"Yeah, I need you go wait outside."

Simon nervously stood on the porch. Every so often, he pressed his ear to the door, hoping to learn something. Without warning the door swung open. Simon backed away, slightly embarrassed. Harriet stepped out onto the porch, gently closing the door behind her.

"So, what is it?" Simon asked, anxiously.

"Well, it seems your little girl is not a little girl any longer. She's with child."

"Are you sure?" Simon posed.

Harriet shot him a look of anger and disgust. "I've been doin' this before all of ya been born. I think I know when a woman's havin' a baby."

She stepped down off the porch, starting toward her home.

"Is she going to be all right? What should we do?" Simon called to her.

"All she needs is rest. If she doesn't, she'll lose the baby," Harriet warned. "When she starts showing, let me know."

"Thank you, Miss Langley."

Harriet didn't answer; she turned and continued on her way.

Simon looked in on Emma. She was fast asleep. He ran back to the field, knowing he'd been away too long

Back in the field, Simon worked his way to Cora.

"Is she all right?" Cora asked anxiously.

"She'll be fine. I had Harriet Langley look at her."

"What did she say? What's wrong with my baby?"

"There's really nothing wrong with her."

"Simon, what are you not telling me?"

He hesitated for a moment. "Emma's going to have a baby."

These words struck like lightening. Cora was speechless.

"That's enough, you two. Move away from each other, and get to work," one of the overseers ordered, poking Simon with his rifle.

****

At the end of the day, Cora and Simon walked home. Neither of them spoke. Simon looked to Cora, seeing the worry on her face, except what could he say to lighten her mood? So, he remained silent.

Sitting on the edge of the bed, Cora reached out, stroking her daughter's forehead. Emma's eyes opened.

"How are you feeling, sweetheart?" Cora asked, smiling.

Harriet had already told Emma of her condition, earlier. The young woman dreaded the moment of confronting her parents.

"I'm so sorry, momma."

"Don't be," Cora whispered. "We love you. Nothing's gonna stop that."

"But I let you down."

"No, you didn't let us down. You're just human, like all the rest of us."

Unable to look her mother squarely, Emma turned her head. "What about Anthony?" she cried.

That was a subject no one wanted to talk about. Powerless to give an answer, Cora said what was in her heart. "It's gonna be all right. We're here for you. Everything's gonna be all right."

Believing what she had to say was important, Emma turned once more to look at her mother. "What about the baby? What if it's...?"

"It's gonna be all right," was the best Cora could say.

Nine

Another Reason to Hate

"If you prick us, do we not bleed? If you tickle us, do we not laugh? If you poison us, do we not die? And if you wrong us, shall we not revenge?" Pastor Jefferies' voice boomed from the pulpit.

The congregation looked up to the pulpit, half of them in awe at Jefferies' elegance; the other half not sure of what was said. Jefferies broke it down for them.

"What I'm saying is that all are made is God's image. He is our creator. We belong to Him. Not even ourselves, let alone some plantation owner!"

"What do we do about it?" someone shouted from the gathering.

"Start thinking like a free man and you'll start acting like a free man." Jefferies thunder.

"That's enough of that!" a voice shouted from the back of the church. Everyone spun around to see Monk walking up the aisle with two gunmen behind him. Each had their hand resting on their holstered pistol. "There'll be no more of that!"

Standing at the front of the church, Monk addressed the congregation. "From now on, no more Sundays off, and no more church, ya hear? Sundays be like any other day, it be a workday." He turned to look at Jefferies. "Pastor, you opened your mouth once too often. Come with us."

"He ain't going nowhere!" someone proclaimed. Monk and the other two men turned around to see Anthony at the front door, aiming his rifle at them. "Now, take your guns out, slowly, and placed them on the floor."

"Ya don't want to do this, boy," Monk warned.

Anthony lowered his aim, firing. The bullet hit no less than a few inches from Monk's feet. Pieces of wood flew up into the air. Anthony brought his aim up, again. "I said to put your guns on the floor."

Slowly, the three did as they were told. The sound of the heavy guns hitting the floor resonated throughout the church.

"Pastor," Anthony called out. "Get the guns, and come with me."

Jefferies stepped down from the pulpit, standing before Monk and his men. "This is not the way to do this, son. He who lives by the sword will die by the sword."

Anthony sighed, shaking his head. The he looked directly at Pastor Jefferies. "You call this living? What would you have me do, Reverend? They're closing down the church, and they want to take you away. Do you know where they want to take you? To your death, that's where. Now, pick up the guns, and come with me."

Jefferies knew Anthony was right. He bend down, picking up the guns, placing two in his pant's pockets, one in the left, the other right. The third gun he held in his hand, oddly enough, he held it by the muzzle, not the handle. He made his way to the front of the church to stand by Anthony.

"The first head I see coming out of this church is gonna get shot off," Anthony declared. "Let's go, Pastor."

Just before leaving, Anthony took one quick look around. He was hoping to see Emma. Sadly, she wasn't there.

Jefferies stood in the doorway. "God bless y'all," he announced to his flock. "Pray for us."

Outside, there were three saddled horses waiting for Monk and his men.

"Can you ride, Reverend?"

"It's been years, but I think I still remember."

In a flash, they were mounted and gone.

At the sound of horses galloping away, Monk ran out of the church, only to see their dust kicking up off in the distance. He reentered the church.

"Everybody out...now!" he shouted.

When they were all standing outside, Monk looked to his two men. "Burn it down," he ordered.

In no time, the congregation was in tears, watching their church go up in flame. The dry old wood went up like a box of matches. Monk made them stand there until it was nothing but a pile of ashes.

****

"If you fail me one more time, I won't fire you; I'll kill you, myself!" Fergus shouted into Monk's face.

"I'm sorry, sir. It won't happen again."

Fergus gave Monk the back of his hand, hard, sending Monk across the room and onto the floor.

"See that it doesn't," Fergus said, as Monk made it back onto his feet.

"Now, listen to me, and listen good. I want that Anthony and that holy man caught. I don't care if you kill Jefferies, But, Anthony, I want him brought back, alive. This time, none of this huntin him down with two or three men, I want you to take half the men with you. And don't come back without him. Now, get out of my sight."

Monk left the main house, rubbing his swollen jaw.

****

Anthony and Jefferies rode hard through the woods, up one side of a mountain, and halfway down the other.

"We've got a good head start on them," Jefferies said. "Why'd we ride so far?"

Anthony began taking the saddles and bridals off the horses. "I wanted to get on the opposite side of the mountain, so we could have a campfire. I'm tired of eating raw fish and rabbit."

The thought of it made Jefferies shiver.

As soon as the saddles and bridals were removed, without warning, Anthony slapped both horses on their rumps. They took off down the mountainside.

"What did you do that for?" Jefferies asked.

"They'll be looking for horse tracks. That will keep them going in the wrong direction for at least another day."

After eating their *cooked* rabbit, the two men sat close to the fire, as the night closed in.

"Anthony, we need to talk. I have something to tell you. It's about Emma."

"Emma?" Anthony yelped, his face washed with worry. "She's all right; there's nothing wrong?"

"Anthony…Emma's pregnant…she's having your baby."

It was as if Anthony turned to stone. He stared blankly into the fire, the shadows dancing across his face.

****

Anthony was right and he was wrong. Letting the horses go galloping by themselves got Monk and his men off the pursuit trail. Only not for as long as Anthony hoped. They found the two horses grazing in a field at the bottom of the hill. Looking back, they could see their campfire glowing in the night, halfway down the mountain.

When they were far enough not to be heard, Monk ordered them to leave the horses, going the rest of the way on foot. They circled the campfire, though far enough to remain in the darkness. Only, Monk entered the circle of light. Taking his piston from his holster, he pressed the muzzle against Pastor Jefferies nose, as he slept.

"Wakey…wakey, Reverend."

Jefferies jumped up, his hands in the air. Within an eye blink, Anthony was awake and on his feet. He grabbed a rifle, aiming it. Monk took hold of Jefferies, placing his pistol to the side of the reverend's head.

"I wouldn't do that, boy."

Anthony remained silent and still as a statue, aiming his rifle at Monk. The other men stepped into the light.

"Put the gun down, boy, or I'll blow your pastor's brains all over this campfire," Monk warned, pulling the hammer back on his pistol. It clicked into place.

"Don't do it!" Jefferies shouted, pushing Monk to the side. The pistol fired, hitting Pastor Jefferies in the neck.

"Go!" Jefferies whispered through the gurgle of blood spouting from his throat. He landed face-down on the ground.

There was no time to take revenge. Anthony turned, running down the side of the mountain. Monk and his men shot at him. Anthony heard the bullets whizzing past him, except it was too dark for them to find their mark.

In time, Anthony came on the horses the men left behind. He released them all, holding the reins of only one of the horses. He shot his rifle twice into the air. The horses ran off in all direction, save for the one he held onto.

Once mounted, Anthony galloped off. As he rode, all he could think of was the face of Pastor Jefferies, as he held his bloody throat. Here was another reason to hate Fergus Malum, another reason for revenge.

Ten

Why Not

"She'll be fine. Just make sure she get plenty of rest and doesn't work in the fields." Harriet Langley warned Emma's parents.

"That's not likely to happen," Simon answered.

"Don't worry," Harriet responded. "I'll get word to Massa Malum. He listens to me. Another child is another slave, which adds to his wealth. He wouldn't want her to lose the child, anymore than he'd want to lose one of his horses. He'll give permission for her to take things slow, once I tell him."

"Thank you," Cora told Harriet as she stepped down off the porch, making her way back to her home.

Oddly, as she was walking away, another slave, a young man approached. Both Simon and Cora recognized him. It was Colby Steward. He was a handsome youth of eighteen. From years of working in the fields, his muscles were large, his body tight. He kept his hair cropped close, just enough to frame his regal looking face. Cora and Simon knew little of him, only the talk about him was always good. There was never a bad word spoke about him.

"Colby...surprised to see you here. What can we do for you?" Simon asked.

"Mr. and Mrs. Tucker, is Emma available?"

"I'm afraid she's not feeling well at the moment," Cora responded.

"Well, I suppose, in a way, I'm really here to speak with you two."

Cora and Simon looked at him, questioning, waiting for the other shoe to drop.

"Mr. and Mrs. Tucker, I'd like your permission to court your daughter, Emma."

It was a very honorable gesture for a young man, still, it took both Cora and Simon off guard. The young man's timing couldn't be worse. Still, it was not something they wanted to discuss with someone not of the family, so they played their part.

"You're intention is marriage, I assume?" Simon asked.

"Colby, you do know her condition?" Cora added. She felt she that needed to be stated, at the least. It was not something you could hide.

"Oh, yes, ma'am. I fully understand, and it doesn't matter to me any. I could learn to love the child just as easily as loving Emma?"

With those words both Cora and Simon understood the entire plantation knew of Emma's circumstance.

"Then you don't love Emma?" Simon asked.

"No, sir, but I assume I will in time. She's a fine girl."

"I respect you for being so honest, but it makes me wonder. If you don't love her, may I ask why you would want to be with her?" Simon posed

"Because I can tell she is lovable. It wouldn't take long to fall in love with her or the child."

"I see," Simon said, thinking it sounded like a good answer, yet, still wondering if it was a good answer. He looked to his wife for advice. She had none to offer. Cora was as thrown off as much as he.

Colby continued, "The Bible says it's not good for a man to be alone. Understand, sir, there are few single young women on this plantation. I've considered them all, and I have to admit, and I'm sure you'll agree, Emma is one of the finest."

Cora and Simon understood his reasoning and his intent, other than that they felt as if wading in deep waters, getting deeper by the moment.

"I'll tell you what, Colby," Simon countered. "I've known you to be a fine young man. I'll have to leave this decision to my daughter. If Emma agrees, then you may have our permission to court her. Go on in, and speak with her." Simon backed away, gesturing to the door of their home. Cora followed suit, backing away to stand with her husband.

Colby stepped up on the porch, walking to the front door.

"Whatever you do, don't upset her," Cora said as he walked passed.

"I won't ma'am."

It was dark in the shack. Emma was on her bed, sitting up with her eyes closes. She was aware of someone moving about, perhaps her parents. When she opened her eyes, she sat up, startled to see the silhouette of a man.

"Don't be afraid. It's me, Colby."

There was a sliver of light cutting across the room. He stepped into it. She became calm, yet remained puzzled.

"Colby, what are you doing here?"

"I was just talking to your parents, outside. They said it would be all right to come in and visit."

"Visit...?" She said, pulling her blanket up, for modesty's sake.

"There's something on my mind that I've been needing to tell you."

Emma moved to the edge of the bed, looking up at Colby.

"I would like you to consider marrying me," he said matter-of-factly.

Emma was lost for word, tilting her head in disbelief. This was not what she expected, and defiantly not what was on her mind.

"I've already asked your parents for their permission to court you. They told me it would be up to you."

"Why?" Emma asked.

Colby smiled. ""Why not? Eventually, both of us will need a mate. How will we know if we're not right for each other, if we don't at least court for a time to find out? Now, I know you were in love with Anthony. I'm sorrow that didn't work out for you. Perhaps, it was never meant to be."

Emma felt relieved. By the way Colby spoke, she knew he knew nothing of her and Anthony being blood related. Still, there were other matters to discuss.

"You do know that I'm having Anthony's baby?"

"Yes I do, and it doesn't matter to me."

"Colby…you're a nice boy. I've always liked you, but I don't think this is the right thing for me to do, at this time."

"How do you know until you've tried," Colby countered. "I'm not asking for anything other than that we spend sometime together, maybe go for a walk now and then, get to know each other. If it doesn't work out, at least you've made a new friend."

Emma didn't seem convinced.

"Please, Emma, give me a chance. I promise, if you tell me not to come around again, I'll leave and never bother you, ever. Please, all I'm asking is we try to get to know each other and become friends."

Emma smiled. It all appeared to be so platonic that it seemed cruel to not say yes. "All right, we can be friends, and you can visit now and then."

Colby's smile beamed at her. He reached out his hand, took her hand and shook it. It was a strange thing to do, a handshake, as if they were sealing a deal. Still, it made her feel comfortable about giving her consent.

"If it's all right with you, I'll come by tomorrow night after dinner. We could maybe go for a walk."

"That would be nice," Emma responded.

"Well then, I'll see you tomorrow," he said, all smiles, as he left the room.

Outside, Cora and Simon resisted the temptation to listen in. When Colby came out onto the porch, they just had to ask.

"So, how did it go?" Simon inquired.

"Just fine, sir, I'll be around tomorrow night, for Emma and me to go for a walk." He sounded pleased with the situation and himself.

"Why wait for after supper? Why don't' you eat with us, and then go for a walk?"

"That's kind of you, ma'am. I'll be here after work."

Somewhere in Cora's mind she figured Colby might just be the thing to get things right again in Emma's life.

Walking off the porch, Colby turned once more to address Cora and Simon. "I don't want to speak against him, 'cause I always like him. But Anthony wasn't right for Emma. In a way, I'm glad he's on the run. I hope he never comes back." He looked at the questioning looks on their faces. "Don't worry. I'm gonna make your daughter love me."

He walked away, feeling cocksure of himself. Leaving, Cora and Simon felt unsure of Colby.

Eleven

Water to Blood

It was the middle of the night, dark, three hours before sunrise. The silhouette of a man moving about the field in the back forty could be seen. That is if anyone were awake to see it. The man rushed through the field bending down every so often, and at other times, reaching to the tops of the cotton plants. He worked diligently till sunup, and then ran back to hide in the woods, watching the goings on from afar.

Fergus and his family were in the dining room, eating breakfast, when Monk came running in.

"Mr. Malum, sir, Mr. Malum…" Monk shouted, waving his arms.

"What the hell's the matter with you, Monk? Can't you see I'm eating?"

"There's trouble at the reservoir, sir."

"What's wrong? It shouldn't be low; we've had plenty of rain."

"The level's high, sir. That's not it."

"Then what the hell is *it*?"

"The water, sir, it's turned to blood."

"Monk, have you been drinking?"

"No, sir, I haven't had a drop since last night. It's true, sir, all the waters turned to blood."

Both his wife and son looked at him, wondering what he would do. He threw his napkin on the table, rose, and started for the door.

"This better be good, Monk."

The Malum Plantation had a large intricate watering system. They had a large and deep reservoir that held rainwater. From the reservoir, there were furrows leading to all the different fields. Opening a levee allowed the field to be watered, being careful not to leave the levee open too long, risking a flooding. It was a good system, and except during droughts, worked well.

Fergus stood on the edge of the reservoir, looking down. It was true. The water was a bright red. He bent down, scooping up some of the liquid in his hand. He took a whiff, there was no odd smell.

"See what I said, Mr. Malum; it all done turned to blood."

Fergus dipped his finger in the liquid in his cupped hand. He pressed his finger against his tongue, giving it a taste.

"This isn't blood, you idiot!" Fergus proclaimed, as he stood shaking the liquid from his hand, and then clapping his hands dry. "Although, it might as well have been, it's clay, red clay, probably from up in those hills," he said, pointing to the hills off in the distance from his property. "Red clay is as good as poison to a cotton crop."

"How did you think it happened, Mr. Malum?" Monk asked.

"Oh, it didn't just happen. Somebody did this on purpose."

"Who would have done this, sir?"

"I think I know," Fergus answered, staring at the hills. "Monk, get buckets, as many buckets as you can get your hands on. Have the slaves empty the reservoir. When their done, have them clean it out. Get rid of all the red clay. Then have them haul water from the wells to fill it up again with freshwater. Now…Monk…I want it done now!"

"Yes, sir, we'll get right on it."

Before walking away, Fergus took one last look at the distant hills. "Anthony…" he said under his breath.

****

It took three day for the reservoir to be emptied, cleaned, and then refilled. For this reason, much of the other work of running a plantation was left undone. Fergus ordered that work hours be extended to make up for lost time.

When they caught up on their work, Fergus demanded that an extra hour would be added to each workday. Now, with Sunday no longer a day of rest, and the additional daily hour, life was bearing down hard on the slaves of Malum Plantation.

Fergus was convinced Anthony was behind the polluting of the reservoir. Fergus warned Anthony that for every act against him that he, with his greater power, would pay back the infraction. Fergus suspected Anthony was in contact with some of the slaves at the plantation. After all, how could one man avoid his men, and do so much damage without assistance? He was wrong. Anthony knew nothing of what was going on at the plantation. This makes you wonder. If he did know, would he cease and desist; or was his lust for revenge so great that nothing would sway him?

Twelve

Life's Purpose

Colby was always a gentleman, keeping his distance, when spending time with Emma. It was becoming a close relationship. As Colby predicted, they became good friends. Nearly every night, they spent time together, often going for walks and talking.

Emma's belly was beginning to show more. There was no mistaking it, now, she was pregnant; it was clear to everyone. It never seemed to faze Colby, which was why Emma felt it best to be open with Colby.

One cool evening, as they sat on the porch of Emma's parents' home, Colby summoned up his nerve. He reached out, taking her hand. It was time to talk.

"Colby, in these past few weeks, I've gotten to know you. And I like you very much. Only, I feel I haven't been fair with you."

He shot her a questioning look.

"You know I'm carrying Anthony's baby. What I have to tell you is for you only. Please, don't ever tell a soul. I love my parents, but my father isn't my real father."

Colby laughed, "What are you talking about?"

"My father isn't my real father," she repeated. "My mother was raped by the Massa. He is my real father."

A look of shock beamed from Colby's eyes.

"And that's not all," Emma continued. "Anthony's mother was raped by the Massa. He is Anthony's true father."

"That makes you…" Colby's voice trailed off.

Emma finished his sentence, "Brother and sister. I had to tell you because of the baby. There's always the chance that…"

"I don't care," Colby said. "I love you, Emma."

Now it was Emma turn to wear a surprise look. Yet, still, why was she surprised. She knew their relationship could end in only three ways. Both of them disillusioned, both of them fall in love, and the worse scenario, only one falls in love.

"I have one more thing to tell you, Colby. Perhaps, it's the hardest thing to say, but need to. I still love Anthony."

"But he's your brother."

"I understand, but that doesn't stop me from loving him."

Colby felt deflated, still he was not dismayed. "You have to come to the realization that you may never see him again. Please, give us more time. Perhaps, one day you'll feel the same way for me, as I do for you."

Emma didn't answer. She was afraid to.

Colby leaned over to kiss Emma. She didn't back away; however, she tilted her head so his lips would land on her cheek.

"I going to go, now," he said as he stood. "May I see you tomorrow?"

"Yes," she replied with little enthusiasm. "Colby, I'm not trying to hurt you. I do like you."

"Emma, you'll probably never see Anthony again. You don't want to spend your life alone. You'll need a husband, and you child needs a father. Think about it."

She knew he was right, still her heart beat fast only for Anthony.

As Colby walked back to his shack, his mind raced with ideas. He came to only one conclusion. Anthony was a stumbling block. In time, if Emma never saw Anthony again, she may consider his offer of marriage. Yet that might take years. He wasn't willing to wait. The answer was simple. No Anthony, no problem.

At his shack, he knelt down at his bedside. Reaching under the bed, he fetched the six-shoot he'd hidden there. Standing, he stuffed the pistol in his belt.

When it was late and all was quiet, he quietly went into the barn. There he saddled one of the horses. He led the stead by the bridle. It wasn't till he was far enough off the property to not be heard, did he mount up.

He rode up into the hills with only one thing in mind, his life's purpose, to find and kill Anthony.

Thirteen

Snakes

It started with the sound of one woman's scream, shattering the peace of the morning. Another woman screamed, then another, and another, followed by the shouts of men. The high squeals of children could be heard. Finally, dozens of slaves were screaming, hollering, and running out of the field. The ruckus was so great and loud, they heard it in the main house. Fergus took his holster and gun down from the wall, putting it on. He thought to himself, *what the hell's the matter, now?*

Fergus came running out, toward the field. He saw a group of slaves standing outside one of the fields, surrounded by overseers. Seeing Monk, he walked up to him, clearly unhappy with the disturbance.

"Monk, what in the hell is going on?"

"Snakes, Mr. Malum. The field is full of `em."

"That's ridiculous," Fergus sneered as he entered the field.

He didn't have to walk far before he had to back out. There were dozens of snakes, all kinds, big and small.

"Anthony," Fergus whispered to himself, knowingly.

In his mind he visualized Anthony traipsing through the woods and streams with sackcloth bags, gathering snakes for days. It would take that long to get so many snakes.

Once he'd collected what he thought was all he could handle, he made his way through the night to the field. Letting the sakes out in the middle of the field, the reptiles were confused and angry, snapping at anything that moved.

One of the overseers came walking up, carrying two shotguns with one under each arm. "Got the guns you asked for, Monk."

"Whoa, what is this?" Fergus asked.

Monk answered, as he took one of the shotguns, "Scatterguns, sir. We can get rid of these snakes in no time."

Fergus believed Anthony placed the snakes in the field to hinder the work, forcing the plantation to lose a full day's work. True to his word, Fergus planned to make the slaves pay, in response to Anthony. Again, Anthony had no way of knowing what was happening on the plantation. This had turned into a war waged in the dark, fought by blind men, of which no one was destined to win.

"That's not the way I want this to go down," Fergus said, taking the shotgun away from Monk, and handing it back to the overseer. Fergus turned to point to the crowd of workers. "I want them to go back into the field and remove all the snakes."

"But, some of them will get bit, sir."

"I don't care," Fergus replied, knowing this was true, and believing it was a way of getting back at Anthony.

"Should we at least give them sticks?" Monk asked.

"No, just their hands," Fergus insisted.

Monk turned to the crowd. "Well, ya heard the man, everyone back in the field to get those snakes."

One of the male slaves stepped forward. "Can we at least spare the women and children?"

"No!" Fergus shouted. He took the shotgun from the overseer, pointing it at the crowd. "I want everybody in that field. I'll kill the first who doesn't enter the field, now!"

Slowly the crowed entered the field. It was clear what they were doing. The men stayed close to the women and children, ready to interact before they were in danger.

A scream echoed from the field, then another, and then another. No one was bit, just the fear of seeing the serpents crawling through the field. Every time someone tried to run out of the field, they were met by the overseers aiming a gun at them. They halfheartedly returned to the field.

The workers were allowed to use long knives for cutting in the fields. The men captured the snaked one by one. Holding the captured snake down under their boot, they sliced its head off. Once a snake was killed, it was brought out of the field and placed at Fergus's feet. In time, there was a pile of dead snakes, amounting to at least fifty.

After hours of hunting and killing, they moved about the field, calmly. It would seem all the snakes had been taken care of.

Suddenly, a high-pitched scream broke the quiet. The next moment, one of the men came running out of the field carrying a young boy in his arms. He laid the lad down on the ground. Using a pocketknife, he made a crisscross cut in the boy's skin over the snakebite on his lower leg. Bending low, he took the leg into his mouth, and proceeded to suck the poison out.

Fergus took his boot to the side of the man's head, hard, throwing him onto his back. "What the hell do you think you're doing?"

"The boy's been bit, sir. I need to suck the poison out."

"You need to get back in that field," Fergus ordered.

The man looked up in defiance and with anger. "No, sir, I won't."

Fergus reached over to the overseer, again, taking hold of the shotgun. He aimed it squarely at the man's face, pulling the trigger. The man was blasted into every direction, a bloody explosion. His body flew five feet back.

"I will kill the fist person to step out of this field without my permission," Fergus shouted into the field, holding up the shotgun.

The lad, who'd been bit, lay on his back, shaking as if having a seizure, as the poison coursed through his frail body. His eyes rolled back in his head. Thick white foam filled his mouth, dripping down the sides of his face. Finally, he took in one long breath, his little body stiffened. He let out the air slowly, and then died.

One hour later, believing all the snakes caught, Fergus ordered the slaves from the field.

"Good work! But since we've lost a full day's work, it will have to be made back up. All of you, back into the field. You will not stop till you make up for lost time." Fergus turned to Monk, "See that they put in a full day's work." Then walk away, toward the main house.

"You heard the man!" Monk shouted.

No one moved, staring down at the child, lifeless on the ground. Fearing trouble, Monk took his gun from his holster, pulling the hammer back. "Now!" he hollered.

Reluctantly, they turned, reentering the field. They worked well into the night, before Monk ordered them to stop. When they left the field, they saw the body of the boy still on the ground. They took the body back to the slave to prepare it for a funeral.

There was much crying by friends and family, as they lowered the body into the ground. Just as the last shovelful of dirt was patted down on the grave, the sun lifted its head over the horizon. It was morning, time to return to the field, time to go back to work.

Fourteen

Gone Rabbit

Fergus was furious with Monk. Now, there were two runaway slaves hiding in the hills that Monk and his men were unable to capture. First, Anthony, and now Colby, more would follow if it wasn't nipped in the bud, immediately.

Colby ran away with one of their horses, a major offense. He was a walking, breathing, dead man. Fergus wanted him destroyed, and Fergus always got what he wanted. This is why what happened next was so peculiar, to say the least.

It was early morning, when the sunlight is just starting to change the dark gray world of night back into gold. A lone ride came slowly up to the main house. Monk and his men saw him coming from afar. Even Fergus saw him from his window. They stood in front of the main house, waiting.

When the horse stopped, all recognized the rider as Colby. Most often, they would have shot him off his mount, but two things stopped them. The amazement in seeing him ride up to the main house without fear. Was he insane? The other was that across the rear of the horse was draped the body of a dead man. Though the corpse was mangled, with closer inspection, it was obvious to all it was the body of Anthony Watson.

Colby dismounted, and walked up to Fergus.

"Massa Malum, don't be angry with me. I know I shouldn't have run off like that, but I knew you wanted Anthony, and here he is," Colby said, pointing to the body slung over his horse.

"I should be mad, but I must admit I am pleased. Why is it that you were able to do what my men weren't?"

"I've known Anthony all my life, I know how he thinks."

"So, you took it on yourself to find him, going without permission, and robbing one of my horses."

"I've returned your horse, sir. And besides, if I asked for your permission to hunt down Anthony, would you have given it?"

"You have a point there. So, tell me why you did this. It certainly wasn't to please me."

"Honestly, sir. I have my heart set on Emma Tucker. She was and still in love with Anthony. I figured if he were dead, she could begin to forget him. I only ask that you tell no one that I was the killer."

"That seems like a fair trade," Fergus agreed.

The men took the body off the horse, placing it at the feet of Fergus and Colby.

"Why is the body so mangled?" Fergus asked.

"I followed his trail for days. I finally caught up with him; he was camped at the top of one of the mountains. I came on him with my gun drawn."

Colby pulled his gun out to show it to Fergus, who took it from him, handing it to Monk.

Colby continued, "I underestimated him. He kicked the gun out of my hand. We wrestled for what felt like hours. He nearly got the drop on me, more than once. Just when he thought he had me, he lost his balance. I pushed him, and he went flying down the side of the mountain. It was some drop. It was nearly an hour's ride to the bottom, where I found him. That's the way I found him."

A thoughtful look came of Fergus' face. He looked at Colby, and smiled. "So, how do I explain you? A slave runs away, steals one of my horses. You bring me the body of someone I wanted dead, but you don't want me to tell anyone. So, again, I ask what I'm supposed to tell these folk. I just forgive you with no punishment?"

"Yes, sir, I'll tell everyone it was out of the kindness of your heart. They will look up to you, and respect you for it."

Fergus shook his head laughing, "That's very inventive, but it's not going to work. If I let you go unpunished, they will think of me as softhearted and weak. What will stop others from running of? No, you need to be punished." He looked to Monk. "Take him!"

Monk and some of the men took hold of Colby. Fergus moved in close, laughing.

"Since you did come back, and you did kill Anthony for me, I'm going to be lenient with you. Normally, when a slave makes a run for it, I have him killed. But since you've done a favor for me; I'm going to do one for you. I'm going to let you live." Fergus back away, looking at Monk. "Cut off his left foot."

"Yes, sir," Monk answered with a tone of pleasure in his voice.

"But, sir...?" Colby cried.

"A rabbit that looses his foot thinks twice about running," Fergus started for the main house. He called over his shoulder, "Some say a rabbit's foot is lucky."

"No...!" Colby shouted as they took him away.

Fifteen

What Really Happened

As Colby rode up the side of the mountain, he noticed tracks and signs left by Anthony. He ignored them. It wasn't Anthony he was looking for. In fact, he did his best to avoid him.

At the top of the mountain, he looked beyond the valley below and the mountain after that. He knew past that was the Abernathy Plantation. This was his goal.

Colby left his horse at the top, walking down to the Abernathy Plantation. At the bottom, he remained hidden in the bushes, observing the slaves working in the fields.

It wasn't long before he saw what he'd come for. There was a handsome young black man, in his late teens, working alone. He was average height and weight, although, there was a familiar shape to him, reminiscent of Anthony Watson.

"Hey, you…" Colby called out in a whisper.

The young man looked around, not sure if he really heard anything.

"Yeah, you…"

He followed the voice to the edge of field. Colby pulled aside the branches of the bush he was hiding behind, aiming his pistol.

"What in tarnation?" the young man exclaimed.

"Come with me," Colby ordered in a low voice.

"What are ya talkin' about?"

Wearing a serious look, Colby pulled back the hammer of his pistol. "Come with me, now! Go on!"

The young man reluctantly entered the underbrush, followed by Colby. They started the long climb up.

"My name is…"

"I don't want to know your name!" Colby snapped.

"I was just tryin' to be friendly."

"Well, I ain't your friend. Just keep climbing."

Looking back, the Abernathy Plantation was becoming smaller, fading in the distance. At the top, they could no longer see the plantation.

The young man looked at the Colby's horse, tied and waiting. "One horse, how we gonna fit on one horse? Where are we goin', anyways?"

Colby pointed his pistol, "Out that-a-way."

The young man looked out. "There ain't nothin' out there."

"Sure there is. Can't you see that?"

"See what?" the young man asked, stepping to the edge of the cliff.

"Right there…!" Colby grunted as he slammed the back of the young man's head with the hilt of his pistol. He went limp. Before he toppled over, Colby pushed him forward. He fell off the ledge. It seemed an eternity before he hit bottom. Colby leaned over, looking down at the lifeless body.

It took half an hour to get to the bottom. Colby took a close examination to the body. It was mangled badly. Taking hold of the head, he turned it, taking a good look at the face. It was bruised and battered; still there were enough facial features to tell it wasn't Anthony. Colby bashed the face multiple times with a sharp rock, hard. When he was done, he examined his handy word.

"Now, your mother wouldn't even know you," Colby whispered to the corpse.

He dragged the body to his horse. It was a struggle to get the deadweight up into position on the back of the mount.

He rode slowly up the side of the first mountain. All along the journey, he continued to go over the plan in his mind, what he'd say to Massa Malum, what he'd say to Emma.

With Anthony out of the way, or at least Emma believing he was dead, there would be nothing to stop him. He would win her for his own, even if it killed him, or anybody else who got in his way.

Sixteen

A Bushel of Salt

There was a light tapping on his front door.

"Who is it?" Colby called out from his bed.

"It's me, Emma."

"Go away."

"I brought you something to eat. Please, let me in."

"I don't want you to see me like this."

"Like what?"

"They took my left foot, Emma."

"I know, I heard. I'm sorry." She waited for a moment, Colby wouldn't answer. She could only image how he felt. She leaned in closer to the door, and whispered, "That's not what makes a man…a man. You're a good man, Colby. Please, let me in," she pleaded.

Emma took his silence as a "yes", and entered.

It was one room, dark. Colby laid on his bed, fully clothed, a blanket covering where his left foot once was. She could see where his leg ended, the blanket dipping down at the knee.

"It's my mama's soup," Emma said, placing the pot on the table in the center of the room. "It'll do you good," she added, looking about for a bowl and spoon. All she found was a chipped coffee mug. She figured that would do, blowing the dust out of it and pouring to the brim.

As she handed him the mug, she sat down on the edge of the bed. He ignored the gesture. She placed it on the nightstand.

"I meant what I said. You're a good man, Colby, be it on two feet or one."

"Would you marry a man with one foot?"

"If I loved him, it wouldn't matter."

"Would you consider marrying me?"

"What do you want me to say, Colby? I'm no way ready to even think about such things. If I say yes, you're gonna wanna get married, I'm not ready."

"That's not what I asked. Would you consider marring a gimp?"

"Don't talk like that," she scolded. "I don't ever want to hear you talk like that."

He felt an urge to say, *Why not, now that Anthony's dead?* But he knew that would be a foolish move. She would need time. Instead, he used it to his own advantage.

"I'm sorry about what happened to Anthony," he said, sounding as sympathetic as he could.

She had heard the rumor that Anthony was dead. Only, the gossip was he was killed by Monk and his men. Fergus Malum had been true to his word. None of the folks in the slave quarters knew the truth.

Emma didn't respond. She looked down at the floor, and gave out a long sigh. Colby thought it best to change the subject.

Colby reached over, taking up the soup. "This is good," he said, sipping at the mug. "Tell your mother, thanks, for me."

"She'll be pleased."

"They say I should be up and around in another week. Of course, I'll have to be on a crutch." He hesitated for a moment. "You wouldn't be ashamed to be seen with me, would you?"

Emma stood up, and walked to the door. "I'll leave the soup. I'll be back for the pot in a couple of days." She stood in the doorway, looking directly at him. "Listen to me, Colby Steward; because I'm only gonna say this one time. I've told you what I think, and I don't want to say anymore. If you want to court me, understand I'll court a man. Now, if your man enough to not let this get you down, then you can court me. If not, then don't bother coming around. Either way, I don't' want to hear this kind of talk again from you"

With that she turned and left.

****

That night after supper, as Emma helped her mother clear the table, Simon left to smoke his pipe outside, on the porch.

"So, how is Colby doing?" Cora asked.

"He's a little down in the mouth, feeling unsure of himself."

"That's to be expected. A man needs his pride, but too much of it ain't good. He'll find his way out of it soon, enough."

"I hope so."

Cora stopped what she was doing. "Why would you say that? He's a strong young man. He'll get over it."

It was clear her mother was standing up for Colby.

"I suppose your right," Emma agreed.

"You know, Emma, I been meaning to talk to about Colby and things."

Emma shot a confused look at her.

Cora continued, "I'm your mother, and I love you. I believe that gives me the right to tell what other folks ain't feeling they got the right to. So, here it goes." She halted for just a moment, took in a deep breath, and then continued. "Anthony is dead. God love him, but he's dead, and he ain't never coming back. He ran away, they caught him, and they killed him. I understand how you felt for him, but it was never meant to be. And even it was, he's dead; you need to move on."

Emma read between the lines. "And moving on means to marry Colby?"

"What would be wrong with that? He's a good man. He'll take care of you. Besides, you're due soon. That child needs a father and you need a man."

"But I don't love him. Not like I loved Anthony."

"Anthony is dead, sweetheart. I'll let you in on a little secret. All these young people who get married think their in love. Well, they're not. They're just starry-eyed. They don't know each other from Adam. You know the old saying; *you must go through a bushel of salt together before you know each other.* It takes time to fall in love, real love, that is."

"Was it that way with Papa?"

"When Simon and I first got married, I though he hung the moon. After a few months, things changed. I sit up in bed, in the middle of the night, looking at Simon snoring away. I'd wonder *who this man that I married is.* I really didn't know him. But in time I got to know him real good. We got to know each other. My love, a true love, grew as the sky. And it's not until recently that my love for him has gotten so deep. I never knew you could feel about another person the way I feel about your father. I think back when I was a young girl, and I just gotta laugh."

"Maybe you're right."

"I know I'm right, sweetheart. Give the man a chance. That's all I'm asking."

Emma smiled and nodded. "All right, I will, momma."

Seventeen

Dreams and Visions

Strange things started happening on the Malum Plantation, concerning dreams and visions of Anthony. Some folks believe that before a soul leaves this world to enter the afterlife, they find a way to say good-bye to certain people in their life.

Whatever the case maybe, there was an uneasiness, a fear, that hung over the entire plantation.

The first person was Emma. She swore Anthony came to her in a dream. She didn't see him, per say; she only heard his voice.

He spoke soft and gentle, his voice coming from the darkness. "Emma, I love you. I will always love you. But now, it's time to move on."

"Oh, Anthony, I love you so much," she called back to the darkness. "I will love you forever."

"And I will love you forever," he replied. "But you must move on with your life, for your sake and our baby's."

"I will never forget you, Anthony. I love you."

"Good. Now, take that love and put it where it will do the most good."

Then he was gone, she felt it. She woke, sitting up in bed; the room was as dark as it was behind her eyes.

"Anthony..." she whispered tearfully, her hands rubbing her belly. The child moved, as if it had had the same experience.

****

Cora was the next to dream about Anthony. It was similar to Emma's dream. It came in the middle of the night. It was just his voice in the dark.

"Anthony, is that you?" Cora whispered, not sounding too surprised. After all, such things happen in dreams.

"Cora, I need your help."

"What is it, Anthony?"

"Emma needs to forget me."

"Yes, I know."

"But, my child needs to know me. Don't let me be forgotten."

"I will tell your child about you. They will know who you are," Cora vowed.

"I have nothing to give them, so give them my name. Call them Anthony."

"What if it's a girl?"

"Antoinette is a lovely name. Will you do that for me?"

"I'll try, but I can only suggest."

"That's all I ask."

As with Emma, his voice faded. Sensing Anthony was gone, Cora woke, sat up in bed, looking around the dark room. Believing in such dreams, she was sure the spirit of Anthony visited her. She would make good on her promise, and speak with Emma.

****

As for vision of Anthony, they were numerous. Many said they saw Anthony, early in the morning, standing in the fields, staring at the slave quarters. Many others said they saw him in the fields in the evening, staring at back at them. Whenever someone brave enough to approach him, tried, Anthony would disappear.

Late at night, his spirit was seen rushing through the slave quarters. He'd weave in and out between the shacks. When called out to, he never responded. When chased after, he'd vanish.

Every morning, a fresh killed rabbit, raccoon, or pheasant, was found on the doorstep of one of the more desperate families. They called this "a visit from Anthony." It meant there would be meat on the table, at least for one night. They referred to Anthony as one speaks of the saints.

****

Fergus ordered Anthony's body (that is, what they thought to be Anthony's body) to be hung from a tree at the edge of one of the fields. This way, all the slaves would understand the consequences of going against him. Though the body was mangled, its conditioned worsened from the birds eating off it for a full week.

Once the body was taken down and buried in an unmarked grave, Fergus wiped the thought from his mind. One would think he would be moved in some way. After all it was his son, except Fergus never thought of it that way. Anthony was no more his son than Ishmael was to Abraham. Isaac was Abraham's true son, as Douglas was to Fergus.

Fergus always believed himself a levelheaded person. If his five senses couldn't detect it, then it wasn't real. However, he began to question his sanity. A face at the window, a voice calling to him down the chimney at night, shadows on the walls, it was all so suspicious. What made it worse was these visions were of Anthony; he was sure of it, though he never mentioned it to anyone. He feared they'd think him mad, or worse, weak.

He'd sit at his desk; open one of the drawers to find a dead animal, usually a rat or a snake. Who would do something like this? Certainly, not Anthony, he was dead.

The voice coming down the chimney at night sounded like Anthony. The voice would call him Papa or Daddy. It was eerie. Fergus would grab his rifle off the wall, run outside, only to find no one on the roof. He'd race around the main house, there was no one there. Then he'd run in the opposite direction, in hopes of catching who it was. That never happened. Back in his study, nervously, he'd pour himself a bourbon.

I was all some kind of sick joke that someone was trying to play on him. When he found out who it was, they would wish they'd never been born.

****

Yet, strangest of all was the dream Douglas experienced one night. The occurrence was no different from the dreams of the others, a voice in the dark. Only, Douglas had no knowledge of Anthony. It was just a stranger's voice.

"Justice must prevail," the voice demanded.

"Who are you?" Douglas asked.

"I am your brother, Anthony."

"But, I don't have a brother."

"We share the same father."

Douglas didn't know what to say to this. The voice continued.

"I am firstborn. I am heir to all that is our father's, you will claim nothing. You will inherit the wind."

This shook Douglas awake. He sat up in bed. In the moment he opened his eyes, he saw the figure of a man standing at the foot of his bed. It was a young black man. Blinking, all he saw was the darkness. The figure had disappeared.

He was unable to sleep. He needed to speak with his father, only he knew his father would never give him a truthful answer, if the voice was right. So, instead of confronting his father, he decided to skirt the issue, and see his father's reaction.

"I had the strangest of dreams, last night," Douglas said, when alone with his father.

"Oh, and what was that?" Fergus asked, not really paying attention, or giving full weight to the statement.

"I dreamed a young black man came to me."

Doulas waited before continuing looking for some sign of interest in his father. There was none.

"He said his name was Anthony, and that he was my brother."

At that moment, his father looked up and into his eyes. No words were needed. By the look on his father's face, he knew he had struck a nerve. He knew it to be the truth.

"That's ridiculous. It was just a fool's dream," Fergus said, leaving the room.

Eighteen

The Other Side of the Broom

They scheduled the wedding for late Sunday afternoon, just after the workday. Emma's closest friends decorated the front of Colby's shack with flowers. Everyone wore their finest clothes, all of them standing in a circle. Colby stood in the center waiting for his bride. Cora stood a few feet away from Colby; she smiled at him, he smiled back.

A tall, lanky man standing at the back of the crowd brought a fiddle to his chin. He began to play a soft, longing tune.

As the first note resonated, Emma, escorted by Simon, slowly marched toward the crowd. When they entered the circle, Simon took Emma's hand, offering it Colby. He took it, smiling at Emma, she smiled back.

Emma looked beautiful. There was a ring of red and white Sweet Williams around her head, interlaced into her hair. She wore a long flowing robe of green that Cora sown for her. She'd worked late into the night, every night for two weeks. Looking at Emma straight on, it was impossible to tell she was with child. Though from the side, there was not mistaking that she was.

No longer having a church or a minister, a return to the old ways were all that was left. Being the oldest in the community, Harriet Langley was to perform the ceremony. She entered the circle, holding a newly made broom that was never used before. She placed it on the ground.

"We're all here to watch these two get hitched," Harriet shouted. The crowed smiled. "That is Emma Tucker and Colby Steward. If anyone knows why these two shouldn't be spliced, say so, now."

The crowd went silent, all wearing the same grin. It was then Cora looked up and beyond the crowd. She saw the image of a young man in the slave's quarters, off in the distance. She couldn't make out his features; only, she would have sworn it was Anthony. When she tried it focus on him, he still was only a vague image.

Cora understood why Anthony's spirit was present. Anthony so deeply loved Emma. She closed her eyes, and said a silent prayer. She prayed Anthony's soul would find peace. When she opened her eyes, Anthony wasn't there. Perhaps, her prayer was answered?

Harriet continued, addressing the marriage couple, "You two, once you jump the broom you'll be man and wife. You understand? You gotta stick together and treat each other right. You ready?"

Colby held a crutch under his left arm; Emma took hold of his right.

"Now, go on and jump," Harriet shouted.

With one quick leap, they hopped over the broom, to the cheers of the crowd.

"You are now man and wife. May you stay together as long as you're owned by the same master or one of you dies," Harriet proclaimed

The circle closed in around the couple, as everyone wanted to congratulate them. They all celebrated, eating, singing, and dancing, into the night. Yet, not too late, as always tomorrow was a workday.

When everyone had left and gone to their homes, Emma and Colby stepped onto the porch of his shack. Colby pushed the door open, and turned to her.

"Forgive me, my love. As much as I'd like to, and as much as I know you deserve it, I cannot carry you over the threshold."

"There's no need to apologize," she whispered, falling into his arms. Then she looked up into his eyes. "If anyone should apologize, it should be me to you."

He understood what she meant. Emma was only days away from delivering her child. There would be no consummation of the marriage, that night.

There's no need to apologize," he echoed her sentiments. Their first night together would be spent in bed, holding each other close.

Nineteen

Plague

There are few things that send fear into the heart of a plantation owner, drought, fire, but plague is the worst. Plague is the most horrible. Droughts will pass, fire comes and goes, but plague is the wrath of God.

There are many, but the two most feared is the Boll Weevil and the Cotton Bollworm. To have both at the same time is an unlikely nightmare. As well, the time of year and for this part of the country was all wrong. It was all very suspicious. You might even say it was intentional. If Fergus didn't know better, he'd suspect Anthony. It was so similar to the snake incident, which he felt Anthony was responsible. Except, he felt positive Anthony was dead. Still, this was what the Malum Plantation was facing, and something needed to be done.

The first thing was to inspect all the fields, and confirm what areas were infested. Thankfully, only a few acres were overrun.

Rows of crop in adjoining fields were uprooted, isolating the plague. A deep, long furrow was dug around the acreage, and filled with water. The infested crop was doused with kerosene, and set on fire.

The branches and cotton buds were aflame in seconds; as well many of the Weevils and Bollworms were burned away.

Still, half of the creatures escaped from the flames. Their only refuge being the water filled gullies around the acreage. The knee-high waters made their get away a slow one.

All the slaves were armed with shovels, hoes, sticks, and planks. As soon as the pests made their way into the water, the workers bashed frantically, squashing them before they could immerge on the other side of the ditch.

It was hard work, and it took hours. When it was over, the channels of water looked gray and murky; the thousands of dead insects floating atop the surface of the water.

They fished the creatures out of the water, placing them on old bedsheets. The water was to remain for a few days, in case some insects were left. Tying the bedsheets, forming large sacks, they toted them to the weigh area. Monk weighted the sacks. Added together, the weight of the plague came to three hundred pounds, and that was not counting the more than fifty percent burned in the fire.

Fergus was angry. Not only was an entire acre of crop lost, but also a full day's work.

"This entire scenario doesn't make any sense," Fergus said to Monk. "Someone did this."

"That's impossible, sir. It was just an act of God," Monk pointed out.

"Oh no, God had very little to do with this. Someone did this on purpose. Are any of the slaves missing?"

"Not a one, sir."

"It couldn't be one of the other landowners. They wouldn't want to start a war they couldn't finish. Tell you what, Monk. Take a small handful of your men and search up in the hills, again."

"...to look for what, sir?"

"...the person who did this, of course."

"Yes, sir," Monk replied. Before leaving, he looked to Fergus. "You know, sir. The slaves, and even some of my men, are saying it's the spirit of Anthony lookin' for revenge."

Fergus stepped forward, just inches from Monk. "If I hear that kind of talk again, from you or anybody else, they're dead."

"Yes, sir, of course, sir..."

Twenty

Mating of Eagles

Beth Harris was the prize of the county. She was young, beautiful, smart, and from a wealthy family. In her late-teens, the only child of Martha and Lawrence Harris, owners of the Harris Plantation, the eyes of all the young men of the parish were on her.

With a slender willowy frame, her dark hair and features likened to models painted by the masters two centuries earlier. Her skin smooth and white like ancient Chinese porcelain, as were her straight white teeth. With emerald green eyes, hypnotic and deep, a smile, warm and friendly, she lit up every room she entered.

There was a beauty of her mind, as well. Often many a young suitor overlooked the splendor of her thoughts. Though frequently, the sharpness of her mind frightened the young men afraid of a strong woman.

As for wealth, the Harris Plantation was not the largest; still, it constituently turned a hefty yearly profit. There wasn't anything her parents could not afford or deny her, though she never became spoiled.

Lastly, her inner beauty was that of a true saint. A warm heart, always willing to give rather than take, to listen, and give of herself, presented her as an angel.

For all these reasons, every young eligible bachelor yearned to be near her, to posses her, falling over themselves whenever around her.

Who can say why two people are made for each other, what attraction pulls them toward each other? Is it magic, chemistry, earthly, or spiritual? Whatever the unknown equation was, it ruled over Beth Harris and Douglas Malum.

Beth and Douglas knew each other since they were children, never thinking twice about the other. Not till a chance meeting at a church social when they were in their teens did they see with new eyes.

There are many different opinions concerning the term *love at first sight*. Some call it impossible, while others stake their lives on it. Notably, the one who believe it, have lived it.

Such was the case of Beth and Douglas. One look from afar, all space between them disappeared. He approached her with confidence, knowing her answer before she spoke it.

They began courting that day. Twice a week, Douglas would ride out to the Harris Plantation. In time, Beth was invited to supper at the Malum Plantation. The visits continued, back and forth, for over a year. In time, the two understood they would one day be married.

Douglas went through the custom of asking Lawrence Harris for his daughter's hand. It was just a formality, a sign of respect. Both Martha and Lawrence saw it coming within the first few months of Beth and Douglas' courtship.

As for their approval of Douglas and their daughter's marriage plans, they were all for it. They liked Douglas from the very start.

In the case of Estella and Fergus Malum, their approval of the marriage was for different reasons. They couldn't care less about Beth's looks or demeanor.

Fergus believed in only two kinds of women, the ones that obey their husbands and the ones who don't. He also assumed that a strong man can handle the latter.

Beth was a strong woman, and if she knew the true nature of Douglas, she would have walked away. Except, people put their best foot forward in a relationship, at the beginning, at least. They keep their true self hidden, sometimes for years. If Beth knew the true Douglas, she would never accept him.

As for Estella, she had no position on matters of the heart. She thought and felt like her husband. The Harris' were wealthy, which would add to the wealth of the Malum family. Power and riches are what matters in life. Love is not necessary. As for the marriage of Beth and Douglas, it would be the mating of eagles.

Twenty-One

Now There Are Four

"Cora, I want you to stay here with me, today," Harriet explained. She turned to Simon, "Simon, tell the overseers, Cora needs me to stay and help me. Emma is having her baby. Oh, and Simon, tell one of the other midwives to come and help."

"Why is there something wrong?" he asked.

"Don't get your feathers ruffled. There nothing wrong. I just want another set of hands. Now, get goin'.'"

Simon looked at his wife, and then his daughter. His eyes were wide, and he clearly broke into a sweat.

"Now…!" Harriet shouted.

"Oh Simon, when you get to the field, tell Colby everything's fine," Cora told him. "Tell him not to come around. We'll let him know when the baby comes. Last thing we need is a nervous father sticking his nose in."

Simon spun around, and nearly pulled the door off its hinges, as he ran out.

"How you feelin', honey? Got any pain?" Harriet asked Emma.

"A little," Emma replied, reclined in her bed, still in her nightgown.

"I'm afraid it's gonna get worse, before it gets better. But don't ya worry. You're a strong girl, and you'll be just fine." Harriet turned to Cora. "I'm gonna need plenty of clean rags, and lots of hot water."

An hour later, one of the midwives arrived. A gray-haired woman named Celia. Harriet was glad it was her. Celia was no stranger to childbirth; she had five children of her own, all grown now. Over the years, as a midwife, she'd helped bring dozens of children into the world.

The morning passed by slowly. Harriet sat on one edge of the bed, Celia on the other, Cora in a chair at the foot of the bed. All eyes were on Emma, her pains increasing every few hours.

Except for the intensity and frequency of the pain, the afternoon was the same, slowly ticking the hours away.

Later in the day, Simon returned.

"What are you doin' here?" Harriet shouted.

"Work is over. I've come home."

"Well, ya can just turn around and go someplace else."

"What about my supper?" he asked.

"Ya selfish little man," Harriet scolded. "Your daughter's havin' a baby, or don't ya care?"

Cora walked to the cupboard, ripped a piece off a loaf of bread, placed a piece of dry beef and a piece of cheese on top. "Here, here's your supper. Now, go," Cora said as she pushed Simon out the door.

"But, where am I suppose to go," he complained.

"What do I care? Go get drunk with Colby. Keep you both busy," Cora said, slamming the door behind him. "Just don't come back until morning."

It was late in the night. All the candles they could find, they kept lit around the bed.

As midnight approached, Emma was in intense and nearly constant pain. Harriet placed her hands on Emma's belly, gently feeling the position of the baby.

"I need to step out and get some air," Harriet announced. "Cora, why don't ya join me? Celia, ya just call out if ya need us."

"That's all right, I feel fine," Cora said, determined to stay by her daughter's side.

"It's gonna be a long night, Cora. Ya need to get some air," Harriet said, rolling her eyes to the door, a clear signal that Harriet needed to talk with her, outside.

"Yeah, I guess I could use a breather," Cora admitted, walking to the door. "Mama will be right back, sweetheart."

The night air was cool and calming. All was quiet. The two women stood on the porch, in awe of the stars spreading like diamonds across the black sky.

"There's somethin' wrong," Harriet said softly. "I can't put my finger on it, but somethin' wrong."

"I thought knew what you're doing? I thought you've done this before?" Cora complained.

"Don't matter if ya done a thousand, they're all different. Just like people are all different," Harriet demanded.

The both fell silent for a moment.

"Is she in danger?" Cora asked.

"I don't know. It just doesn't feel right. The baby's not lined up like it should. I fear the child's sittin' in the wrong direction."

It lay heavily on Cora's heart. She felt the need to say what she never spoke about, except to Simon and Emma. This was life and death. It was no time for secrets any longer.

"This is Anthony's baby," she whispered, as if she wanted no one to hear.

"I know that," Harriet scoffed.

Cora decided the best course was to come right out and say it. "Emma and Anthony are brother and sister."

"What?" Harriet questioned.

"Simon ain't Emma's real daddy. And that ain't all of it. Years ago, both Edna Watson and me were both raped and by the same man. They're brother and sister. Emma and Anthony are brother and sister."

Cora let out a long sigh. As if she'd run a race, she began to shake and sweat.

"Let me guess," Harriet said. "Massa Malum be the father."

"How did you know?" Cora asked Harriet.

"I've seen it all my life. Massa been havin' his way with this one and that. It ain't nothing new. A good bit of some of the folks on this here plantation is his kin. But ain't never known two to have a child, together."

"I'm so afraid," Cora answered back. "This ain't natural. It's against the will of God. Can't we do something?"

"What would ya suggest?" Harriet countered.

"Ain't there a way…" Cora stopped midsentence, afraid to hear the words spoken out loud.

"Tell me, again, about what's natural, and the will of God," Harriet said coldly.

Cora looked away in shame.

Harriet reached out, placing her hand on Cora's. "Now…now, don't go beatin' yourself up about bein' scared. You're only human."

Cora found new steadfastness in Harriet's words.

"I think I know what needs to be done," Harriet said, going back inside. "Cora, ya got any fresh eggs?"

"Why, yes," Cora replied, sounding confused.

"I'm gonna need one."

Harriet sat on the edge of the bed, taking hold of the hem of Emma's nightgown. "I just need to take a look at your belly, dear."

Cora handed Harriet an egg. Harriet held it over Emma. She cracked the shell. The raw egg landed on the top of Emma's stomach. The yolk remained on top, as the rest of the egg dripped down.

Harriet pointed to where the egg dripped the least. "That it…! The baby's head is pointing in that direction. We gotta turn it around. Cora, ya got any cooking oil or bacon grease?"

Cora handed over a small clay pot. Harriet smelled it. It was beacon grease. She took some in both hands.

"Have no fear, child, this is gonna hurt a little, but everything's gonna be all right," Harriet whispered to Emma.

Using both hands, Harriet greased Emma's stomach, massaging forcefully. Emma let out a cry of pain.

"That should do it," Harriet said. "Cora, get me another egg."

This time the egg dripped equally in all directions.

"We did it," Harriet proclaimed.

****

When Simon opened the front door, a sliver of morning sunlight entered the shack. The ray moved across the floor, then up onto the sleeping Cora. She stirred, opening one eye. Simon starred in.

"Simon, are you drunk?" she whispered.

"Only did what you told me to do," he said, using one foot to take off one shoe, then the other foot to take off the other shoe. He looked to see Harriet and Celia asleep in chairs next to the bed. Emma was in bed, asleep, a swaddled baby in her arms. "So, how did it go?" he asked, softly.

Cora opened both eyes. "When you left, there were three women, now there are four."

"Is the baby all right?" He hesitated for a moment. "You know what I mean?"

"Yes, the baby's fine."

He walked over to their bed, falling on it, face first. "Wake me in an hour. I have to get to work."

"You can just wake yourself."

He sat up in bed, knowing that if he closed his eyes he'd sleep for hours. If he missed work, he'd be in a world of hurt.

"What's its name?" he mumbled. "What's the baby's name?"

"Emma and I decided on Annette."

"That's a nice name," he said, yawning.

Cora pointed to the door. "Now, get yourself out of here. Find Colby and tell him he's a daddy of a baby girl. And don't neither one of you come back till after work. I'll have something cooked. You can both see the baby, tonight."

It took a long time for Simon to put his shoes back on. The sunlight cut through the room when he opened the door. The room fell back into darkness when he closed it. Cora closed her eyes, hoping to get some sleep before the baby woke.

Wistful

Twenty-Two

Appear and Disappear

Monk and his men returned a week later, empty-handed and clueless. This did not put Fergus at ease. In fact, it angered him. Something was wrong, and he needed to know what.

Meanwhile, plans for Beth and Douglas to marry were being discussed. The families alternated supper parties at each other's home. Hours were spent discussing the details. A June wedding was agreed on. Being the largest and more central of the two plantations, the wedding and reception would be held on the Malum Plantation. Through his influence, Fergus procured the Bishop Waltham to perform the ceremony. To insure the reception would be grander than anything ever offered in the county, both families would contribute equal sums. The finest food and drink would be served.

Beth, with her mother, Martha, and her soon to be mother-in-law, Estella, would be in charge of the flowers, the dresses for the bridesmaids, and of course, the bride's gown.

Beth and Douglas were to pick the bridesmaids, the groomsmen, the ushers, and of course, the maid of honor and the best man.

It was all planned down to the last detail. What could go wrong?

****

Emma and the baby settled in nicely at Colby's home. In time, everything seemed normal. Every morning, Emma and Colby would drop the baby off to be in the care of Harriet, who was too old for fieldwork. They'd work the day, returning in the evening, collecting the baby. Emma would cook supper. After eating, the family would settle in for the night.

Antoinette was a lovely child. Cherub like, with fat round cheeks, a circular little mouth, plump arms and legs. She wasn't a fussy baby, and was soon sleeping through the night, to the delight of all concerned, including neighbors.

Because of whom Antoinette's true parents were, the night she was born, the women inspected her, carefully, even going so far as to count toes. It would seem that physically she was fine. Still, weeks later, the sword of worry hung over Emma.

Often she would test the child. Tickle her, she'd laugh. Move your finger from left to right, her eyes would follow. Snap your fingers, she'd turn in that direction. Emma would sigh; give a prayer of thanksgiving, only to be overcome with worry within a few days. Then she would repeat the test, thankfully, to the same results.

Living with Colby was not the joy Emma hoped it would be. He never mistreated her or the baby. His cold, distant ways were perhaps crueler. He seemed to be melancholy no matter what was happening around him. He worked in silence, he ate in silence; he'd sit for hours alone sitting on the porch, never saying a word. The talkative young man that courted her seemed to have disappeared. It was he was consumed with thoughts other than what was needed at the moment. Something consumed him, day and night.

At first, Emma assumed he was still overcome with the loss of his foot. It would be understandable. Perhaps, the knowledge that Antoinette was Anthony's child and not his, weighted down on him. Emma felt that too was possible, especially by the way he would stand over the child, staring at her without emotion. Or perhaps, which would be worse, he regretted marrying her. She did not understand his moods. All she could do was be a good wife, and trudge on, which she did.

****

It had been months since Emma dreamed of Anthony. Life was so hectic, she rarely thought of him. When she did, it was fondly and deeply, but life can sometimes get in the way of your living.

The best they could provide baby Antoinette was a heavy quilt and a few blankets on the floor. The child slept peacefully.

Colby nestled to one side of the bed, his head buried deep into his pillow.

It was similar to the last time she dreamed of Anthony, only this time there were no words. In her sleep, somewhere behind her eyes, she saw the dark shape of Anthony enter the bedroom from the window. He stood over the child, looking down upon her, his face contorted in pain.

Bending low, he scooped the child up in his arm. He held her close, looking at her sleeping face. There were tears in his eyes.

"What is her name?" he asked.

"Antoinette," she replied. "We named her after you."

He gently placed the baby back onto her quilt.

"I'm sorry it turned out his way," Emma said.

"Don't be," Anthony said. "It's the only way it could have turned out." He looked at Colby, fast asleep. "Does he treat you well?"

"Yes, he does," she replied. It was the truth, just not the full truth.

Anthony started for the window. "Are you happy, Emma?"

She ignored the question. "I miss you, Anthony."

"I miss you, too," he said, staring at her for a moment, and then he turned and was out the window.

It was like the last time. She wasn't sure if it was a dream, a vision, or was it real. The last thing she remembered was crying herself to sleep.

****

The day for Beth and Douglas' wedding was fast approaching, only one week away. The Saturday before, everyone in the wedding party was gathered at the Malum Plantation for a wedding rehearsal. Everyone, that is, except the Bishop Waltham. He couldn't be expected to take away from his busy schedule for a simple run-through. It was nice enough for him to agree to perform the ceremony, the following week.

There would be six bridesmaids, in all. Emma's cousin Thelma Ruskin was to be the maid of honor. There would be an equal about of groomsmen, with Bret Brooks as Douglas's best man. Bret and he had been best friends since elementary school.

There'd be five ushers, all of them male cousins from both sides of the family. Four-year-old Kristine Ruskin, younger sister of Thelma Ruskin would be the flower girl. Three years old, Bo Carver, Monroe Carver's son was to be the ring bearer.

Of Course, Lawrence Harris would walk his daughter down the aisle. Right up to Douglas, who waited nervously.

It was such an awkward moment, that it slowly turned into a comedy, everyone laughing, which was easier to swallow by all.

Martha and Fergus sat off to the side, as spectators, pleased not to have to be in the center of the chaos. When they finished, they repeated the ceremony six more times, till in its natural state it held beauty and dignity.

Fergus ordered food and drink to be served as a picnic with table and chairs. The food was nothing that would be served for the wedding. You save the best for last. Still, summer barbecue is a treat.

One of the bridesmaids placed a tiara of Sweet Williams around Beth's head. She looked like an angel.

"You look beautiful wearing those flowers," Douglas said, stealing a kiss.

"I need to freshen up," she said, kissing him, and then walking toward the main house. It went without saying that she would use Douglas room.

Once everyone was seated and the food was served, they began eating.

Fergus jumped to his feet. "Hold on, hold on, we've forgotten something."

"Don't tell me you want to say grace," Martha called out. Everyone had a good laugh at that.

"No, that's not what I mean. We need to wait for the bride."

It was true. There was an empty chair next to Douglas.

The guests kept themselves entertained with conversation and jokes. There was much laughter.

Estella leaned over to her husband and whispered, "The food's getting cold."

Fergus looked to his son. "Douglas, go see what's taking her."

Douglas ran to the house; inside, he flew up the stairs.

"Beth, sweetheart, you need to hurry. Everybody's waiting," he called out as he rushed to his room. The door was open. "Beth, honey…" he called out, as he entered. She wasn't there.

He assumed that they somehow past each other, and she returned to the others. He was just about to leave the room when something on the floor caught his eye. One the floor was the crown of flower, the Sweet Williams that one of the bride's maids placed upon Beth's head. He reached down, taking it with him.

Returning to the others, Douglas held up the tiara. "Has anybody seen Beth?" Few paid attention. "Anybody seen Beth?" he repeated, this time shouting.

"We thought she was with you," someone called back.

At first, no one showed much interest. However after minutes passed by, an air of confusion and concerned covered the gathering. Eventually, guests were searching the grounds. Fergus enlisted some of the house slaves and a few of the overseers to help in the hunt.

"This isn't like her," Beth's mother said, nearly in tears, her voice and hands shaking with worry.

After nearly an hour, they concluded dire measures needed to be taken. The women would remain at the main house, while the men would saddle up and search the area.

Finally, after hours of no results, they gave up the search, and returned to the plantation. The sun was nearly down when they arrived.

Douglas was half hoping Beth was at the main house, waiting, that it all had been some kind of mistake. Only, she was not with the women.

"I'm not giving up," Douglas declared. "I'm going in for a change of clothes and supplies, and then I'm going back out to look for her."

"Count me in," answered some of the young men.

"I'm coming, too," both Lawrence and Fergus declared.

When Douglas rushed out of the house, he found his father handing out guns to the men.

"Monk...!"Fergus called out. "See that the women get home, all right."

"Yes, sir..."

"Father, do you think guns are a good idea," Doulas asked, worried.

"Son, guns are always a good idea."

Twenty-Three

Stare Into the Fire

In a blink, the world went black. Beth was in Douglas' room, standing in front of the mirror, taking the Sweet Williams from her hair. Then suddenly, a sack was thrown over her head. Her next instinct was to scream, except before she could, a hand clamped across her mouth. Immediately, she knew it was a man's hand, large and strong. His arms wrapped around her, carrying her off.

She sensed being taken down the stair and out of the house. Then she was thrown over the back of a horse. He mounted, and they were off. They rose slowly up into the mountain; she could fell the angle.

It was night when they stopped, she could tell by the sounds and smells. He hauled her over his shoulder, seating her down on the ground. Though she wanted to scream, she saw no reason to make a sound.

He made a fire a few feet in front of her. She could hear the crackle of the flames and feel the heat.

When he pulled the sack off her head, she opened her eyes. Blinking, the world was not much brighter than with the sack on. The only light was from the small fire at her feet. Looking around she knew she was in a cave. The sound of footsteps over stones made her turn to look. entering into the light was a tall, young black man.

Beth refused to show any fear. She braced herself, sitting up, addressing him, "Who are you and what do you want?"

He lowered himself down, sitting cross-legged next to her. "You hungry?" he asked. "I hope you like rabbit, because that's all we got."

Beth was determined not to breakdown. "If you think because my father's rich, you can kidnap me?"

"I wouldn't call this a kidnapping. Besides, I don't want your daddy's money."

"Then what do you want?"

He thought about this for a second. "I'm no sure. I don't know. I only know what I don't want."

"And what don't you want?"

Anthony just smiled. "What's your name?" he asked.

Beth continued, "Listen, they're probably out looking for us, now. They'll kill you, when they find you."

This made Anthony laugh. "I'm sure you're right."

Anthony reached over, took hold of a skinned rabbit on a skewer, he held if over the fire. "I hope you like your meat well-done. It's the only way I can eat this stuff, rodent, that is." He seemed to take pleasure in announcing they were having rodent for supper. He looked to see if it made any kind of impression on her. It didn't.

"I'm not afraid of you?" she said.

"That's good, because that wasn't my intention."

"Then what is your intention."

He smiled, "I don't think I'm going to tell you."

When the rabbit was done, he offered her some. She refused, ignoring him.

After eating, Anthony lie on his side to get some sleep, he urged her to do the same. Only, sleep would not come; her mind was racing.

More than once throughout the night, when she felt certain he was in a deep sleep. She rose from off the ground, only to be caught by Anthony, who seemed to sleep as light as a spider's web.

"Where are you going?" he'd ask.

After three failed attempts to escape, exhausted, finally, she gave into sleep.

****

Day's went by, neither one of them spoke much. Anthony kept Beth at his side at all times, even when he hunted, or gathered wood. Beth tried on more that one occasion to run away. Only, it was useless. She was no match for him. He was faster and stronger. He'd race after her, grab her, and carry her back. Though he was firm with her, he never hurt her. In time, she gave up on the thought of running off.

After two days on a hunger strike, Beth decided to eat. Again, it was like most nights, the menu was rabbit, squirrel, or some other small forest animal.

Without looking at her, in the middle of a chew, Anthony spoke, "I'm doing this for hate's sake. I have nothing against you."

"Then who are you against?" she asked. "Who do you hate?"

He took a long time to answer, "My father..." he said solemnly, after a swallow.

"What do I have to do with your father?"

Again, a long pause, "Fergus Malum is my father."

A shocked look washed over Beth's face. However, she wasn't born yesterday. It took her a few minutes, and then after putting two and two together, she understood. "Mr. Malum is your father?"

Anthony didn't give her a direct answer, still she understood she'd hit the mark.

For the next hour, Anthony told his story, confirming Beth's suspicions. Yet, he left out the part about him and Emma being siblings, only that their love was doomed because of Fergus Malum.

"I have nothing against you," Anthony told her. "It's my father that I want to take revenge on."

"What about your brother?" Beth asked. "Does he deserve revenge? He's the man I swore to marry. He's a good man."

"You honestly believe that, don't you?" he asked.

"Of course, why shouldn't I?"

Anthony just shook his head and laughed. "So, what's your story? Tell me about yourself."

Beth laughed, "You're kidding, right?"

"No, I'm serious. I'd like to know."

Beth told her story. It was what was to be expected, far from Anthony's story of woe. She'd come from a wealthy family, well educated, churchgoing, loved babies and horses. One other interesting fact was though her family owned a plantation, which meant they owned slaves, she was deeply against it. Many a family argument around the dinner table was of her arguing with her father.

"Have you ever discussed the matter with your fiancé?" Anthony asked.

"No, now that you mention it, we've never spoke on the matter. But I'm sure Douglas feel the same way. He has a very big heart."

Anthony shook his head, a smile on his face, "You should ask him, someday."

"Oh, so you're not going to kill me?" Beth asked.

"No, I'm not going to kill you."

****

It was a strange phenomenon. Within a week of being together, solely, Beth and Anthony settled in with each other quite well. They would talk for hours. Beth would accompany Anthony on his walks to fetch water or check on the many traps he setup in the area of the cave. She would also help collect firewood. In time she got to appreciate the taste of well cooked rabbit.

Every night, after eating, they'd stare into the fire, and talk. It was mostly small talk, though sometime delving into the deeper subjects of life.

A bond formed between the two, which was why Beth felt confused by what Anthony said to her, one night.

Anthony stood in the mouth of the cave, holding a long piece of rope.

"I'll be gone for a few hours. I won't be back till late tonight or early morning. I need to tie you up."

Beth didn't say a word. She looked at him, as if she never knew him.

After he tied her hands behind her and her feet together, he walked to the opening of the cave.

"I'm sorry I had to do this. It's the only way."

Again, Beth remained silent. This was worse than if she had cursed him out. As he walked down the mountain, all he could think of was his regret for what he was doing. It placed a great weight on his heart. He was temped to turn back, untie her, and ask her forgiveness. Nevertheless, his thoughts of hated and revenge at Fergus Malum, his father, weighed on him more.

Twenty-Four

You Didn't Run

It was too dark to make out features, yet it was still possible to make out shapes. Clearly, there was the shape of a man off in the distance, making his way to the reservoir.

True, Todd Burins, everyone called him Toddy, was not the sharpest knife in the kitchen. When he saw the figure moving, instead of inspecting, he ran to the bunkhouse to wake Monk.

"What the hell are ya doin' here, Toddy? Ain't ya supposed to be on watch?"

Ever since the mischief happening on the plantation, a night watchman kept vigil throughout the night.

"There's somebody movin' around in the fields by the reservoir," replied Toddy.

"Damn it, Toddy, do I have to do everything on this here plantation. You're as dumb as an anvil."

Monk dressed quickly, and took his rifle. The two men ran off to the fields. Hunkering down, Toddy pointed across the field to the reservoir. "Look, there he is! Do ya see him?"

They could make out the silhouette of a man standing on the edge of the reservoir. There were twelve water block in the reservoir, each entering a channel feeding into a different field. The man opened the first block. They could hear the water rushing, filling up the field. When watering a field, you opened the block just long enough to fill the channel, which would be enough to water the field. That's all that was needed, and then you close the block. It was clear this man had not intentions of stopping the water's flow. He wanted to flood the fields.

When the man moved to the next block to open it, Monk stood up, aimed his rifle and fired. The bullet hit the man in the shoulder, sending him flying. Monk and Toddy ran to the reservoir, only they were too slow. When they got there, the man had already run off. They quickly put the block in place, but it was too late. The field was flooded. Acers of cotton plants were ruined.

****

Anthony struggled through the pain, rushing up the mountainside, holding his bleeding shoulder. Luckily, the bullet went clear through, no bones were broken, and it was not lodged in his shoulder.

The sun was up when he reached the cave. Entering, he came on the rope he'd tied Beth with; it was lying in a pile, she was gone. He got down on one knee, taking up the rope to examine it. Again, there was that heaviness in his heart. He dropped the rope to the ground. A sound made him look up. Beth entered the cave, carrying an arm full of wood to replenish the fire.

Smiling when she saw him, and then it disappeared when she saw his bloody arm.

"Your arm!" she shouted rushing to him. "What happened?"

"I took a bullet. It's not bad, it went clear through."

"We have to clean it or you'll get infected. Take off your shirt."

He did as he was told. She heated up some water, and with a few clean rags she cleaned the wound. Then she bandaged the injury, as best she could.

"Thank you," Anthony said slowly.

"Does it hurt?"

He nodded. "No, not really..." He looked her in the eye. "You didn't run?"

She looked up into his eyes, wearing a small, soft smile.

As natural as the sun or the moon moves across the sky, their faces moved toward each other. Their lips met, and they kissed ever so passionately. Her arms wrapped around his neck, pulling him down. His full weight on top of her, his arms encircled her waist. The morning birds were singing.

Twenty-Five

I Hate You, You Know

The days flowed easily, one after another, filled with long hours of unspeakable joy; yet everyday passing too quickly. Beth and Anthony grew closer, wanting to go on together, forever.

Oddly enough, if either one of them thought about the past, a feeling of guilt would take hold of them.

Thinking of Douglas, shame would wash of Beth. She was his fiancée, which in its own right was a form of an oath, and she was breaking it.

Reflecting on Emma and the baby tortured Anthony. Even though he knew it was never meant to be, he felt he was doing something wrong.

"You know, we can't keep playing house, like this, not in a cave, that is?" Anthony said, one evening, hold Beth in his arms, her head resting on his chest. The flames in the fire were dying, causing them to sink slowly into the darkness.

"Then let's go somewhere else," she said dreamily, her eyes closed.

"There is no place for us," he replied.

She quickly sat up, looking at him. "What are you taking about? We'll go someplace faraway."

He lifted himself up on his elbows. "Everyplace faraway is not different from here. Think about it, Beth, a runaway slave and the daughter of a plantation owner. There is no place for us."

"Of course, there is. There must be," she cried. Tears were running down her cheeks.

"No, Beth. The world is not ready for the likes of us. They will catch us, and when they do, they will kill you because of me."

"And they will kill you because of me," she softly agreed.

"I love you, Beth, with all my heart, but this has to end. You must leave in the morning."

He hated to say it, and she wanted so much to argue the point. Still, she loved him and would respect his decision.

She brought her head back down, resting on his chest. "Anthony…make love to me."

***

Neither one of them slept through the night. A sliver of light peered into the cave. The sound of larks outside, warned of the morning.

"It's time," Anthony whispered.

Beth gave no reply.

They dressed in silent. There was not need to eat anything, the though of food was not foremost on their minds.

Outside, the sunlight was beginning to show over the horizon, giving just enough light to make out shapes.

Anthony pointed to the down side of the mountain. "Just head in that direction, always following the sun, keep it to your back in the morning, in front of you later in the day. You should make it by late afternoon."

They stood face-to-face. Beth's tears ran down to and off her chin.

"I hate you, you know?" she said, in a quivering voice.

"I know you do," he said, taking her in his arms, causing her to cry all the more. "If there was a way…" he left the thought unfinished.

They backed away from each other, slowly. Beth closed her eyes for a moment and turned. Opening her eyes, she started down the mountainside, not looking back.

Anthony stood, watching till she was gone from sight. The tears he'd tried so gallantly not to show, for her sake, now, welled up in his eyes, and ran down his face.

Twenty-Six

Original Sin

It was nearing the end of the workday. Toddy was in front of the main house. He was to deliver the day's weight count of cotton to Fergus. For a moment he looked off to the left. He saw someone walking down the road, coming closer. He stopped, his eyes squinting, straining to see who it was. As they came closer, he realized it was a woman. Even closer, he recognized her.

"Mr. Malum….Mr. Malum!" he hollered, running to the main house.

Monk heard the shouting. He ran to the main house. He got there just as Fergus appeared on the main house porch.

"Toddy," Fergus s shouted, "what the hell's the ruckus all about?"

Standing before the porch, Monk behind him, Toddy pointed down the road. "Missy Harris, sir, Beth Harris is comin'."

Fergus focused on the woman heading for the main house. He recognized her as soon as Toddy said "Beth Harris". He stepped off the porch, shouting up to the second story, "Douglas, get yourself down here. Douglas…Douglas…Douglas," he repeated at the top of his lungs.

Douglas appeared on the porch. He looked to his father. Fergus pointed down the road. At a glance, Douglas knew it was Beth. He jumped off the porch, running to her.

"Beth, darling!" he called out to her.

When he reached her, she fainted, collapsing into his arms. He took her up in his arm, carrying her to the house.

****

Beth opened her eyes to find herself lying in bed, in Douglas' room. Douglas sat in a chair, bedside, holding her hand.

"Don't move, darling," he said, when she tried to sit up. "You need to rest. You've been through a lot."

Beth relaxed down onto the bed. There was a knock at the door, it opened, Fergus entered

"Mind if I come in?" he asked, not bothering to wait for an answer. "How do you fell, my dear?"

"A little weak, but I'm all right."

"Well, I won't take much of your time. I have a few questions to ask you, if you don't mind." Fergus took Beth's silence as a yes. "Do you know who kidnapped you, and do you know where he is now?"

"He was one of your slaves. His name is Anthony. But he's long gone, now. He let me go days ago. He said he was heading north on the Underground Railroad. I imagine he's many miles away by now."

"It took you days to get back?"

"I got completely lost. It was by sheer luck that I got back."

Fergus seemed content with Beth's answers.

"We've sent word to your parents. They should be here soon to collect you. Thank you. I leave you both to it."

Fergus turned and left.

Douglas takes Beth's hand once more. "Beth, darling, this may not be the right time to ask this, but I need to know. Did he take advantage of you?"

It was an awkward question, although, Beth though it to be a reasonable one. After all, they were still engaged.

"No, Douglas, he never took advantage of me. He probably wanted to get ransom money for me. Something went wrong. He let me go, and he ran off."

Douglas looked relieved, dropping his head in her lap. She gently stoked the top of his head.

True, she loved Anthony more than any one she'd every known, with a love she never knew was possible. Still, there was a place for Douglas in her heart.

"I was so worried," Douglas sighed. "As soon as you feel up to it, we'll start talking about the wedding, again."

****

"We have a situation," Fergus spoke privately in his office to Monk. "Colby lied to us. It seems we were duped into believing Anthony Watson is dead. I don't know where he got that body, but it wasn't Anthony."

"I'll have my men take him, immediately," Monk declared.

"No, so fast," Fergus replied. "Colby will be punished, but not for lying to us."

"I don't understand, sir."

"If these people find out that Anthony is still alive, others may try the same. As well, I don't want any heroes, giving them hope. No, I want them to continue to believe Anthony is dead. We'll capture him in time. As well, if we do anything to Colby for hoodwinking us, we'll look like fools. We can't have that. We will execute Colby in front of everyone, but not for his original sin. This is what I want you to do."

****

Early the next morning, before sunup, Emma and Colby lay in bed, sleeping, as did the baby.

Without warning, Monk kicked in the front door, followed by three other men. The noise woke Emma and Colby. The four men stormed into the bedroom. Colby sat up in bed. The baby began wailing. Emma rushed to Antoinette, taking her in her arms.

"What's this all about?" Colby shouted.

"We got word you've been stealin'," Monk shouted back. "Go on, boys."

The three men began ransacking the entire house. Starting in the kitchen, they took everything that wasn't nail down and tossed it to the floor. They looked in every cupboard, emptying the contents to the floor. When the kitchen was completely demolished, they started in on the bedroom.

One of the men got down on his knees, looking under the bad.

"I found it," declared the man, as he stood up, holding a full bottle of fine bourbon whiskey.

"I never seen that bottle in my life," Colby insisted "You planted that there."

Monk took the bottle from the man, examining it. "This is from Mr. Malum's private collection. Take him."

"I ain't never robbed nothin'!" Colby shouted, as they carted him away.

Emma stood, crying, before Monk. "Please, there must be some mistake."

"Yeah, and your husband made it," Monk laughed. "Just be glad we don't take you with him."

Monk turned, walking through the kitchen, kicking everything out of his way. He didn't even bother to close the front door behind him.

Antoinette was crying louder, now.

"Hush, Antoinette, momma's here."

Twenty-Seven

Don't Give Up Hope

There is an ancient African saying: *One lives, one dies, the land prospers.* Death on a plantation was as common as birth, in someways perhaps more. Slaves on the Malum Plantation accepted death like the weather, it comes, it goes, and always unpredictable.

Colby's execution would be a merciful one, a simple hanging.

All slaves were gathered to witness. A rope, a horse, a tree was all that was needed.

No speeches were made, not a word was spoken. Although whispers abound as to why the powers that be demanded Emma and her child to be present. Why was it necessary for her to watch her husband hanged? To them, this was crueler punishment than the hanging; especially to a woman all knew to innocent of any crime. The only saving grace was the child was too young to know what was going on.

It was a pitiful sight to see Colby, his hands tied behind his back, two overseers at his sides, helping the one footed man hop to his death.

The horse stood under the large oak. It was a struggle to get Colby atop the horse. Once they did, they placed the noose around his neck.

Colby and Fergus' eyes locked.

"I ain't never robbed anything!" Colby shouted for all to hear. "I am an innocent man." Deep within he knew this was a lie. No one is innocent, least of all him. He'd die with blood on his hands.

He felt tempted to yell the truth to all. That he was being executed for outsmarting Mass Malum. Except, the thought of losing the love and respect of Emma stopped him, especially since there was only a few minutes left.

He looked over to Emma and the baby. She was crying. She was the only one crying. The look on his face was sad, his eyes begged for forgiveness.

Monk stood before the horse, smiling.

"Don't I get any last words?" Colby asked.

The smile grew on Monk's face, and then he broke into a fit of laughter. "Ya coloreds really crack me up. Ya never had permission to open your mouth, all your life. What make you think now is any different?"

Monk nodded to one of his men. He slapped the horse on the rump. The beasts leaped forward, leaving Colby dangling at the end of the rope.

Colby's first reaction was involuntary kicking. He bounced on the end of the rope like a child's toy. The sound of him choking and gasping for air filled the atmosphere. No one could hear or see anything else. The bouncing became more pronounced and higher, which was a blessing in disguise. The movement was so violent, his neck snapped. The sound of bones cracking was loud enough for all to hear. Colby went silent and motionless, his body swaying like a pendulum. The world went silent. One by one, the slaves walked away, some were crying, and all heads were bowed.

"You and the baby need to come home with us," Cora whispered to Emma. "They're not gonna let you live on your own. You're gonna have to come back home with your father and me."

"I know, mama. The baby and I will be over tomorrow. I want to spend at least one more night in our home."

"You sure that's a good idea?" Cora asked.

"We'll be fine, mama, see you in the mornin'."

Antoinette quietly slept in Emma's arms. Emma walked back to her home in a daze. She never understood loneliness like she did at them moment. First, Anthony, and now Colby, it all seemed so hopeless and pointless, until, she looked at Antoinette sleeping in her arms. There still was meaning to life. She couldn't put it into word; still, she knew it to be true.

The floorboards creaked under her, as she walked up the stairs of her home. Strange, the front door was slightly ajar. That wasn't like her to leave it open.

Entering the first room, she stopped in her tracks, freezing like a statue. In the center of the room was the figure of a man. There was not nearly enough light to make out his features, only his form.

Moving forward, his face became clear. Emma didn't know if she was dreaming. She couldn't be. Perhaps, it was a vision, a glimpse of the other side. The man standing before her was Anthony.

The room began spinning, her mind swam, and then the world went black.

****

"Where's Antoinette?" was the first words out of Emma's mouth, when she regained consciousness.

"She's fine. She's on her quilt, sleeping," Anthony told her.

Emma was in her bed. She sat up, staring at Anthony. "I don't understand…I…" She was truly lost for words.

"It was all a mistake. They found a dead body; they thought it was me."

Anthony felt it best not to say anything about Colby being part of the deception. What good would it do now? The man was dead. Emma lost a husband. He saw no reason for her to lose more than she had already. The truth may hurt at times, and is not always necessary.

"I'm sorry about what happened to Colby," he said softly.

Emma's face went blank.

Anthony looked over at his sleeping daughter, admiring her beauty.

"She's fine," Emma said. "She's a healthy, happy baby." She somehow knew this was a question foremost in his mind. He was not only pleased to hear that, but also that she took away the burden of having to ask.

"What will you do now?" he asked.

"We'll move in with my parents, we've got no choice. What will you do?"

"I'm not sure. I…" his thoughts trailed off. He looked down at Antoinette. "May I hold her?"

Anthony leaned over, gently taking the child up in his arms. Antoinette remained asleep. He couldn't take her eyes off her, as he spoke.

"I have to go. I will be back, soon. There's got to be a better life for you and Antoinette. I don't know where it is, but I'll find it. When I do, I'll be back to take you there. Just stay strong, never give up."

Anthony placed Antoinette back down. He went to the bedroom window, and opened it.

At that moment, Emma's heart was breaking. In her mind, she couldn't find a place for Anthony. He was no longer her fiancé. She couldn't bear to think of him as her brother. All she knew was that she loved him.

"I love you, Anthony."

"I love you, too," he replied.

That was as far as either one of them would go.

With one leg already out the window, he turned one last time to her. "Don't give up hope, stay strong. I will be back for you."

With that, he jumped out the window, running for the forest.

Twenty-Eight

On Purpose

What makes a plantation different from a farm is that a plantation is self-sufficient. The workers not only live and work on the property; they grow and raise most of their own food, and make their own supplies.

Besides slaves and overseers, the workforce needed to run a plantation, animals play a large part.

On the Malum Plantation, there were two chicken coops, housing hundreds of chickens, raised for their eggs and for meat.

A large grassy field was put aside for cattle. From these they got milk and meat. A dozen slaves were in charge of milking the cows, daily.

Behind the barn was a pigpen. Fergus liked his bacon.

As well, they kept a small kennel of dogs, good for security, hunting, and chasing down runaway slaves.

Lastly, there were the horses. Different horses for different jobs. Huge muscular horses for labor, plowing and carting, sleek fast horses for riding, and animals of beauty to pull the carriages.

The care of these animals was foremost, even before the care of slaves, as they were considered more essential and far more costly.

It was an ordinary morning on an ordinary day. The kitchen staff in the main house was up and at it early, breakfast for the Malum family. The first thing to prepare was the item that took the longest to make, that would be the biscuits. The secret to a good country biscuit is to make sure the ingredients are fresh. This was easy, seeing how, besides the store-bought flower and sugar, the milk, from which butter was also made, and eggs, all were fresh from the plantation.

"Nanna, smell this milk," one of women asked Nanna, the head cook

She walked over, dipping her head down, inches above the bucket of milk. "Hmm," she moaned, sounding hesitant. She put her finger into the liquid, placing it in her mouth. "It's off."

"Sour?" asked the girl.

"No, not sour, off, somehow."

"Nanna, looky here!" shouted one of the other girls, pointing at the bottom of a large bowl.

Nanna walked over, her gaze followed the girl's finger. At the bottom of the bowl was an egg she'd just cracked. The yolk was black as a lump of coal.

"That a bad sign, an omen, somethin' bad is gonna happen."

"It's just a bad egg, you stupid girl," Nanna warned. "Throw it out and crack another one."

The girl did as she was told, only the next egg was the same, a black yolk. "Looky, looky," the girl shouted. "The devil done got into the henhouse."

Nanna pushed her aside, cracking one egg after another. Each time was the same, greenish whites, coal black yokes. She leaned over and took a whiff. "Smells as bad as it looks," she proclaimed.

Nanna took the bowl of spoiled eggs, left the kitchen, and headed for the dining room. There she found Fergus, alone, drinking his morning coffee. Strange thing was, as she entered through one door. Monk entered through another.

"Mr. Malum, sir, all the dogs at the kennel are sick, some of them are dead!"

Fergus jumped to his feet, starting for the door, followed by Monk.

"Sir, I need ya to see this," Nanna said, holding the bowl out to him.

"Not now, Nanna! I got problems."

"Ya do need to see this, sir," she insisted, pushing the bowl in front of him.

Fergus looked into the bowl. "What the hell is that?" he shouted.

"Eggs, sir, all the eggs are that way."

"The dogs, sir," Monk persisted, thinking sick dogs more of a problem than rotten eggs.

Fergus shoved the bowl back at Nanna. "Wait for me in the kitchen. I'll be back soon."

Fergus and Monk stood by the kennel fence. All the dogs, two dozen of them, lay on the ground. Most of them were dead; those still alive were struggling to breath.

Without saying a word, Fergus ran off toward the back of the barn, closely followed by Monk.

Standing at the fence of the chicken coop, it was worse. There were hundreds of chickens on the ground, dead.

Again, Fergus ran off, persuaded by Monk. At the fence, the cattle looked strong and well, as did the swine. Fergus wasn't an expert by any means, but all was quiet, and they looked healthy.

It was the same in the barn. All the horses were standing straight and tall, looking healthy.

"Take my horse, it's the fastest. Ride into town. Tell Doctor Morrison to get here, pronto. You understand?"

Without so much as a "Yes, sir", Monk saddled Fergus' horse, and was galloping toward town.

Three hours later, there was no sign of Monk or the doctor. Finally, in the sixth hour, a buggy came wheeling up to the main house. It was Doctor Morrison and Monk.

"What happened?" Fergus demanded.

"Sorry, sir," Monk said. "I got about a mile from out of town, when suddenly the horse fell over dead. I had to walk the rest of the way."

"So, what's the problem, Fergus?" Doctor Morrison asked, getting out of the buggy.

"Don't rightly know, Doc. I got a kennel full of dead dogs, and a coop full of dead chickens. And now I learn my best horse's is dead, too. We need to check the barn."

Entering the barn, they found half of the horses lying on the ground. Morrison checked a few of them, some were dead, and the others were dying.

"What is it?" Fergus asked.

"I don't know," Morrison replied, "but if I had to guess, I say that this is not a disease, not an illness. More like something they ate."

"The chickens, too," Fergus complained.

"I know, that is strange since chickens don't eat what horses do. Let's go check on to the cattle."

The field was covered with dead or dying cattle. As for the pigs, they were all dead, except for a small litter of piglets.

"This is going to take me hours to figure out, maybe a day or two," Morrison claimed. "Fergus, go back to your home, make sure nobody eats or drinks anything from this plantation. Monk, you do the same with the workers and slaves. Nobody is to eat any meat, no eggs, and no milk. Not until I get a handle on this."

****

It was early the next morning when Doctor Morrison came to Fergus in the main house. Morrison worked through the night, investigating the cause of all the ill and dying animals.

"Fungicide," Morrison said point-blank. "It's deadly poisonous, when people eat it. Usually, animals are immune to it, except in very high doses. All the grains you've been feeding your animals have a high level of it. This fungicide is made from mercury. I guess you could say they died from mercury poisoning."

"This…this fungicide…how did it get in the grains?" Fergus asked.

"There's only one way," Morrison replied. "Someone had to put it there. This was done on purpose."

"Anthony…" Fergus whispered under his breath.

****

In the empty field where they kept the cattle, Fergus ordered a large circle dug in the center of the field, away from the fence and road. Monk and his men oversaw the event. On Doctor Morrison's order, they worked with bandannas tied across their faces, as to not inhale any of the smoke. Morrison wasn't sure but he feared taking in Fungicides, even as a fume, might be dangerous, maybe lethal.

All the male slaves were made to carry all the dead animals and put them in the circle. They too wore bandannas across their faces. Some of the slaves had to be whipped into submission, afraid to touch the caucuses.

"There was poison in their feed, twasn't no disease," Monk announced loudly. "Touchin' any of these beasts ain't gonna make ya sick. I'll shoot the next man who doesn't do what I say!"

It was a massive pile of death, dogs, bulls, cows, swine, and chickens.

Doctor Morrison took Fergus off to the side and into his confidence. "I'd make sure all the animal feed is taken away. Don't touch it, though. Use shovels, you hear. Then go buy other healthy animals to replace these, and replace all the feed."

Fergus took Monk to the side. "This was the work of Anthony, I'm sure of it. Take two or three of your men, go up into the hills and find him. Do not come back until you have him, dead or alive."

After the sound of Doctor Morrison's buggy riding off, and the sound of Monk and three of his men riding across the fields toward the mountains, was the sound of kerosene being poured over the dead.

It was a foul smell mixture of kerosene and spoiling flesh. A match was lit, and tossed in the center of the circle.

In the blink of an eye, flames rose to the sky. The caucuses caught fire like weeds on the threshing floor.

There was the smell of chard meat, like some Southern barbecue from hell. The air was sweet with the smell of death.

The sun was taking one last bow before leaving the stage for another day. The play was over. The curtain fell on another act. There were no flowers for the ingénue. No standing ovation. No call for "Author, Author", just a draped blackness and a flame that lit up the sky yellow and orange. Folks said they could see it from the next county.

Twenty-Nine

Puppies and Kid Goats

That Sunday, after church, knowing their predicament, the Harris family invited the Malum family to a lunch at their home.

Martha Harris reached across the dining table, placing her hand atop of that of Estella Malum.

"Estella, you poor dear, what you're going through, I can only imagine."

"I've ordered and purchased new animals and feed, we should be back up to snuff in three to five day," Fergus said gruffly.

"Well, if there's anything you need, in the meantime, just ask," Lawrence Harris declared to Fergus.

"Thank you, Lawrence, you're a good friend."

"I suppose this will postpone the wedding," Martha declared, looking at Beth and Douglas.

Douglas took hold of Beth's hand. "Just a little while, Mrs. Harris, we'll be rescheduling soon."

Everyone at the table smiled at hearing this, except Beth. Though she hated to admit it, the thought gave her a feeling of relief.

"Do you know who might have done this?" Lawrence asked Fergus.

"No, but I have my suspicions. We have a runaway slave named, Anthony Watson. At first, we though he was killed. New information tells us he's alive and well, and hiding in the hills. I've sent some of my men after him. I told them bring him back dead or alive, and don't come back till you do."

It was a good thing no one looked at Beth at that moment. She wore a worrisome look, as her heart went out to Anthony.

"It's a shame," Martha declared, shaking her head.

"It all my father's fault," Douglas announced.

Everyone stopped eating; all eyes fix on Douglas, waiting for the other shoe to drop.

"We have this argument, my son and I," Fergus said. "It seems my son thinks I'm too softhearted with my slaves."

"You…lenient?" Lawrence scoffed.

"It's true," Douglas said. "He treats them too well, for slaves. You have to pay a man to work. A free man you give money. A slave gets paid in fear and pain. The more money you give a free man, the harder he will work. The more fear and pain you give to a slave the harder he will work."

"I pity the poor black bastards, when I'm dead and gone, and Douglas takes over the plantation," Fergus laughed. They all laughed along, except Beth.

"It will be a better world, when I have my way," Douglas proclaimed.

****

"Is that how you truly feel?" Beth questioned Douglas, as they walked the Harris Plantation, after dinner.

"Truly feel about what?" Douglas asked.

"About the way you'd treat your slaves."

"Oh, that," Douglas laughed. He took hold of her hand, and laughed louder. "You shouldn't worry about such things. These are things men are more apt to handle. There's no need to worry your pretty little head over such stuff." He stopped walking, turning her to face him. "I know how women think," he said. "You've all such big hearts. You think of slaves the same way you think about puppies and kid goats. They're just cute creatures to y'all. Just leave men's work to the men."

He leaned over, kissing her on her cheek. They turned to walk on, hand in hand. She stared off to the hills off in the distance. Somewhere out there was Anthony.

Thirty

Three in Blue

Anthony stood at the top of the second hilltop from the Malum Plantation, looking back at the hilltop behind him. There, atop the far off peak, Anthony saw a small group looking like a cluster of ants on an anthill. There was no doubt in Anthony's mind that it was men from the plantation on the hunt for him. His only hope was to move forward, keeping the lead he had on them, and making it even more so.

Going downhill was easy. He often ran whenever he came on a section with few to no rocks. It was the same with the valley. Going uphill was slow and difficult. Still, he kept moving forward. After twenty-four hours of none stop trudging, he had a large lead from his pursuers. He'd gone past to where he'd be sure they would not go any farther, believing he would stay close to the Malum Plantation. He was far off in another county.

On the third day of his journey, late in the evening, Anthony saw a campfire glowing in the valley below. It must have been a mile or so away. As he approached it, he was cautious with his footing, not to make noise.

He came upon a large rock. Climbing the side of the rock, he stayed well hidden, yet he was able to hear what they were saying. From the sound of their voices he could tell they were all men, and there were three of them.

"Do we have any more beans?" asked a deep voiced man.

"Here ya can have mine," said a younger, thinner male voice. "When I get out of this outfit, I ain't never gonna eat beans again."

"Beats starvin'," said a third voice.

"Yeah, well, maybe."

Anthony inched higher up the rock to where he was almost looking over it.

"The hell with this, I'm gonna catch me some sleep," announced the second voice.

"We need to backtrack goin' east, tomorrow," said the deep voiced man.

"Yeah, whatever…"

Anthony moved up slowly, peering over. The campfire was bright, glowing on the three men, giving Anthony the surprise of his life. The three men were dressed in the unmistakable blue Union soldier uniform. Finding three union soldiers in this county was an oddity, in itself. What was even more striking was that all three Union soldiers were black men.

Anthony's inner voice told him to move on, only there was a part of him that wanted to know more, and that made him believe he'd be safe.

The rustle of Anthony's feet through the dry leaves on the ground was a sounding alarm. Before he stepped into the light of the campfire, the three soldiers were on their feet, guns in hand.

"Put down the gun, now!" shouted the deep voiced soldier.

Anthony placed his rifle and pistol on the ground, along with his shoulder bag.

"Now, raise your hands in the air."

Anthony complied.

"Now, who the hell are you?"

"My name's Anthony Watson."

"And that supposed to mean something to me?"

"He's a runaway! Can't you tell?" the thinner, younger man said.

He walked over to Anthony, picked up his shoulder bag, and began rummaging through it.

"Say, what we have here?" the younger man asked, taking a piece of meat from the shoulder bag, and holding it up to see.

"It's some cooked rabbit," Anthony said.

The young man held it under his nose. "Heavenly…" He took a bite. "Ambrosia," he said with a full mouth, chewing. "You can put your hands down, now. Want to join us for dinner?"

Anthony shrugged, not knowing how to answer.

"Sit down," continued the soldier. "You like beans?"

****

"I'm John…this is Sergeant Paul Turner, and this big guy is Big Jim. And your name, again, was…?"

"Anthony."

"Right…so, tell us where you runnin' from, and where to are you runnin'?"

"I'm from the Malum Plantation, a few miles south of here. I'm going to…" He had to stop, when he realized he had no clue where he was heading. "I got family back on the plantation. When I find a safe place, I'm going back for them."

"You're a mighty long distance from a safe place, my friend," John laughed.

"Look who's talkin'" Sergeant Turner laughed, as well. "They catch him; they kill 'em. I'd hate to think what they'd do to us, behind enemy line."

"Tell me, where you fellas from?" Anthony asked.

"Massachusetts, Volunteer Infantry. Got separated from out troop, been tryin' to find them for two days, now."

"I ain't never seen black soldiers before," Anthony said.

"Oh, there's enough of us," Turner replied. "Our entire troop is all black, except the commander."

Big Jim ate the last bit of rabbit, tossing the bones into the fire. "Ya know, maybe we can help ya with finding where to go."

"That's a whole day's walk from here, in the wrong direction," John protested.

"I know," said Big Jim. "But, I say we help the kid."

"What you talkin' about?" Anthony asked.

"The Underground Railroad," Big Jim replied.

"There's a train that takes on slaves?" Anthony asked, wide-eyed.

The three soldiers laughed.

Sergeant Turner took it from there. "No, that's just what they call it. It's a line of safe places goin' from the south to the north, mostly farms."

"Where is this railroad?" Anthony asked, his voice pleading.

"We know a safe place. They'll know where to send you next," Big Jim answered back.

"Hold on one stinkin' minute. Did ya not hear me say that it's in the wrong direction?" John protested. "I say point him in the right direction, and say a prayer."

"I'm the highest ranked here," Turner pointed out. "And I say we take him."

"Great! That's just great!" John grumbled. "I just hope they hang you first, so I'll have time to say, *I told ya so*."

"Get some sleep, kid," Turner told Anthony, as he rested his head on a log, pulling the brim of his cap down over his eyes. "We'll take ya in the morning."

Thirty-One

About Us

The distance grew between Beth and Douglas, although Beth was the only one of the two that notice. Douglas was oblivious to the change. Perhaps, the reason he did notice was because Beth did not acting any different toward him. All changes were happening in her head. Not only were her feelings for Douglas waning, but her feeling for Anthony increased, to the point where she thought of him constantly. Missing him deeply threw her into a deep depression.

As she learned more about Douglas, especially his treatment of slaves, she felt more uncomfortable around him. Often, she'd find reasons to not be alone with him.

Still, there were times being alone with Douglas was unavoidable. After all, there were wedding plans to be made. The wedding was scheduled for the early fall, when the temperature is tolerable.

It was an evening supper at the Harris Plantation. Both families were gathered, as well as a few other prominent families from the area. There was much eating and drinking, laughter, and embarrassing humor focused on the young betrothed couple.

Everyone understood when Beth and Douglas left to take an after dinner stroll. After all, young people need to spend time alone, to discuss, to dream, to spark.

Beth felt uneasy, as they walked in the dark, hand in hand.

"I'm counting the days, my love," Douglas whispered, expecting a response. When there was none, he pressed her, "Are you all right, darling."

Beth was so lost in thought; it took her a moment to realize he was talking to her.

"Oh, yes. Sorry, I was just thinking."

"About what?" he asked.

"About us," she replied. This was the truth, only not in the way Douglas would believe. She wanted to run away. Except, to where and how? There were so few alternatives for a woman. A woman must marry; this was understood by family and community, without being spoken. If she didn't marry Douglas, at some point she would marry another young man from the parish, and they were all the same, all of them like Douglas. The dream of being with Anthony was just that, a dream. He was gone out of her life, forever. If Anthony ever did return, that day would be his last.

It was dark at the back of the house. Douglas stopped, turned to her, spun her around, and toke her in his arms. His mouth pressed hard on hers.

"Douglas, you mustn't. Someone will see," she whispered, pushing away from him.

He pulled her in close, again. "They're all inside. No one will see us." He placed his lips to hers.

It was true. No one would see them. She had no reason to protest, so she submitted. Yet, it was more of being kissed than kissing.

Without breaking free, he spun her around, pushing her up against the house, pressing his full weight against her.

"Douglas, no..." she moaned, trying to break free.

He ignored her; now, his hands were upon her.

Douglas, please, stop."

"What's the difference; we'll soon be married."

"Douglas, please..."

He continued, paying no attention to her plea. She wriggled as hard as she could, twisting her head to break free.

Douglas pulled away. Before she could give out a sigh of relief, he gave her the back of his hand. She began crying.

"I'm sorry, Beth. But you have to understand who going to wear the pants. A man has needs."

She wiped a small trickle of blood from the side of her mouth. She stopped crying, when she looked at the red on the back of her hand.

He took hold of her arm, dragging her around the building. "Never mind," he said. "You've ruined the mood, anyways."

At the front door, he stopped before entering.

"Straighten yourself," he ordered.

Beth fixed her dress, and then ran her fingers through her hair.

"Now...smile," he commanded.

She forced a smile. He opened the door. They entered. At that moment, Beth understood what the rest of her life would be like.

Thirty-Two

Safekeeping

It looked more like a fantasy dream than a real home. A one-story cottage covered in whitewash, ivy climbing the walls, beds of red roses all around, encircled by a white picket fence. There were lace curtains in all the windows, a curl of grey smoke rose from the red brick chimney. Not far from the house was a red barn, sturdy and newly painted. The farmland that was all around was plowed with the meticulous order only a mathematician's mind could conceive. The order of it all is what made it look so unreal.

There were workers in the field; black and white, men and women. Clearly, none of them were slaves.

No one paid any mind to the three soldiers with Anthony, as they opened the gate, walked to the cottage, and knocked on the front door. An elderly white woman stood in the doorway. She was dressed plainly, but orderly, same as her surroundings. She smiled when she recognized the three soldiers, and called out to her husband.

"Jacob! Those three soldiers from last week, they be back."

Her husband stood beside her. He was a large man, both tall and wide in the chest. He had the look of every biblical figure ever written about. His hair was white, both on his head and his long beard, although his mustache was shaved away.

"I didn't expect to see thee again. Didst thou get lost?"

"No, sir," Sergeant Turner replied. "May we come in, sir?"

"Thee are welcome," he answered, moving aside, gesturing for them to enter.

The inside of the home was plain, clean, with the same orderliness.

Sergeant Turner made the introduction, "Mr. and Mrs. Helfer, you've been so kind to us, already, I feel bad about asking for another kindness. We found this young man; he's a runaway, he needs to hop a train. You are the only ones we know who can help him."

"What is thy name, son?" Mr. Helfer asked.

"Anthony Watson, sir."

He turned to his wife. "Molly, prepare food and drink for our guests."

"Thank you, sir," Turner said. "We need to get going. We'll leave Anthony in your safekeeping."

"Molly, give these men a loaf of bread and some cheese for the road."

She smiled, going to the kitchen. Meanwhile, the three said their good-byes to Anthony.

"Ya take care, ya hear," John said, shaking Anthony's hand.

Big Jim took Anthony by the hand, "If you're ever in Boston, ask around for Big Jim Bailey." They both knew they would never see each other again. Still, as they say, it's the thought that counts. It was a noble gesture.

Sergeant Turner placed his hands on Anthony's shoulders. "Godspeed, son, stay safe. I pray it all works out for you."

"Thank you, all of you," Anthony said.

Just then, Molly returned with a sack. She handed it to Turner. "There's a loaf of bread, some cheese, and a few bits and pieces I had around. Forgive me, I wish it was more."

"Thank you, ma'am," Turner said, taking the sack.

Jacob held the door open. "Go with God."

They left without looking back. Anthony felt the need to say more, only nothing came out.

"Well, young man, if ye need to board a train, thou will need a ticket." He shouted out from the open door. "Joseph!" A moment later, a dark haired white man with the longest, thickest mustache Anthony ever saw, came running up.

"Yes, sir…"

Jacob bent low, whispering in the man's ear. The man shook his head, looked at Anthony for a moment, and the turned, running off.

"Molly, this young man looks to be in need of sustenance," he announced, closing the door.

Thirty-Three

Minty

It was a good life. After a week, Anthony nearly forgot all his trouble. As long as he remained busy, his mind would be calm. Late at night, waiting for sleep to take him away, his mind would wander back to his woes, his thoughts haunted him. He'd pray for the ones he loved. The faces of Emma and his daughter would float before his eyes, behind his eyelids, as he lay in bed. But it was Beth who came to him in his dreams. They were in the cave, holding each other before the fire. When the fire died, he'd wake. Beth would be gone, but the image of her lingered.

Mr. and Mrs. Helfer were good people. They gave him bed and board for his labor, working alongside others in the fields. As well, they gave him a salary. It wasn't much, but to receive pay for your efforts makes a man feel free, makes him feel he's a man.

At the end of the workday, Anthony was done it. Still, it made him happy to be so tired. There are two types of tired. When you slave for another, it kills you slowly, and the tired at the end of the day is a part of that death. When you are paid for you labor, you finish the day tired, also. Only, it's a good tired. It's a blessing running through your entire body. A tired that makes you smile and sleep well.

It was midafternoon; Anthony was in the fields with the others. He enjoyed the work, able to talk and laugh with those beside him. Being appreciated, the atmosphere, and the acceptance made him work all the harder

Looking from the field, up the road leading onto the farm, they could see two figures coming closer. When they were a few yards away, it was clear only one of the figures was human. One was a donkey that had seen better days, its back carrying supplies. A tangling coffeepot clanked and clanged as it moved. The other figure was an old black woman. It was clear she had seen better days, as well. She was small, frail, gray, and hunched over. They moved slowly, stopping in front of the Helfer cottage. The woman tied her donkey to the fence, and made her way down the walkway to the front door, where Mrs. Helfer met her. The two women embraced, and then disappeared into the house.

One of the workers next to Anthony remarked, "Minty…"

"How's that…?" Anthony responded.

He pointed in the direction of the cottage, as he spoke. "Minty, that's her name," he explained. "Well, at least that's what they call her. Don't know much about her, only that she used to be a slave, and now she's free. She shows up here, every few months. That's all I know."

"Quit flappin' your jaws," the overseer hollered.

"She's got somethin' to do with the Underground Railroad. She's connected with it, somehow," he finished his thought.

They resumed their work, although Anthony couldn't help wondering, staring at the house and the donkey.

****

At the end of the workday, on his way to the bunkhouse, Anthony was stopped by Mr. Helfer.

"Anthony, I've come to ask thee to sup with us tonight. What say you?"

"I would like that, sir. Let me wash up and I'll come right over."

Mr. Helfer smiled, "There be someone I'd like ye to meet," he nodded, and walked off.

Anthony didn't ask, however he felt sure, the invite had something to do with the old woman who arrived that afternoon.

Mrs. Helfer answered the door. "Anthony, it is good to see thee, enter…enter."

At the dinner table stood Mr. Helfer, with him was the mysterious old woman. Entering the room, Anthony felt relieved when she smiled at him. He smiled back, she nodded slightly.

Mr. Helfer made the introduction, "Minty, this is the young man we told thee about, Anthony Watson. Anthony, this is Minty. Sit everyone, be at peace."

After saying a lengthy grace before dinner, they settled into their meal. Anthony sat across from Minty.

"How old are ya, son?" Minty asked.

"…nineteen, ma'am."

"Nineteen," she laughed. "I got shoes older than ya."

The others laughed, as well. Anthony smiled, shrugging it off, with a touch of youthful embarrassment.

When the laughter died down, Minty's face went deadly serious.

"So, Anthony, you want to take a ride on the Underground Railroad?" Minty asked.

"To me honest, ma'am, I'm more concerned with my family. I'd like to see them live someplace safe."

"Where are they?" Minty asked.

"A plantation just west of here, the Malum Plantation..."

"I'm familiar with it," Minty said. "How many are in your family?"

"Just two," Anthony responded. "There's Emma and my daughter, Antoinette."

Jacob laid his fork and knife down. "Son, did thou not say they wife and daughter?"

Anthony bowed his head slightly. "Yes, sir, we were never married. We had our child out of wedlock, for which I am truly sorry."

"A sin such as that, like all sin, the Lord will forgive, if thou confess with thy mouth. Though still, thou should make an honest woman of her. It's only right you marry the mother of your child."

Anthony lowered his eyes in shame. "I can't," he confessed.

"But thou must," Jacob insisted.

"I can't...because..." Anthony stopped, his hands were shaking and tears flooded his eyes.

"Leave the boy alone, Jacob," Minty said. "I think I understand." The old woman reached across the table, taking Anthony's hand in hers. "I lived most of my life as a slave on many plantations. I wasn't freed till later in life. I got to see it all. Don't be ashamed. I've seen this many times. You learned too late, didn't you?"

Anthony nodded.

"Let's just concentrate on getting your Emma and daughter out of there."

She let go of his hand, reached into her pocket, pulled out a folded sheet of paper. She unfolded it, sliding it to Anthony. She pointed at it, as she spoke.

"This here is the Malum Plantation. This is the second mountain north of there. I have to be north of here, to help another. I will meet you on that mountaintop, one week from today. We'll get your Emma and Antoinette a ride on the Underground Railroad."

Thirty-Four

Cold Ash

They replaced all the animals and feed on the Malum Plantation. Still, it would be weeks before order was restored. Knowing this, out of the kindness of her heart, Martha Harris put together a basket of food to be taken to the Malum home. One of the overseers was to deliver it by wagon.

"I'd like to take the food to them," Beth asked her mother. It was an understandable request. It would be a chance for Beth to see Douglas. After all they were engaged, they were in love, weren't they?

"Of course, you can, dear," her mother agreed. "I'll just tell the overseer…"

"No, that won't be necessary. I'd like to go alone," Beth replied.

"I don't think I like the idea of you going alone,"

"Now, mother, you know I can handle a buggy as well as any man."

Her mother thought for a moment. "I'll agree to it on one condition. You take one of father's small pistols with you. You can keep it in your purse."

"Mother…" Beth complained.

"Don't mother me. You go with a pistol, or you don't go at all."

****

As Beth brought the buggy onto the Malum Plantation, heading toward the main house, she saw Douglas. He hadn't seen her. He came from the main house and started walking toward the heart of the plantation. She called out to him, except he was too far away to hear. She tied the horse up in front of the main house. Leaving the food in the back of the buggy, she followed him.

Her full dress made it impossible to catch up with him. She was always out of ear shout. He was moving quickly, past the fields, till he was in the slave quarters. He knocked on one of the shack doors. It opened, he stepped inside.

Beth could think of no reason Douglas was there. She tiptoed up the front steps, standing on the porch; she put her ear next to the door.

She heard a young woman's voice screaming, "No, no, stop, please."

Whoever it was sounded terrified. Beth gently opened the door, stepping in. Inside was dark; it took a moment for her eyes to adjust.

It was a small one-room shack with beds along the walls, a small table in the center of the room.

At first, Beth saw no one. She looked about the room – no body. Moving forward, she saw Douglas on the floor, his back to her, under him was a young black girl. She couldn't have been more than sixteen, if she was that. She struggled to break free of him, pleading with him.

"Massa Douglas, stop, no…"

"Douglas, what are you doing?" Beth questioned, standing next to them.

He was so deep into his passion, he didn't hear her.

"Douglas, stop it!" she shouted, taking the pistol from her purse, pressing it against his temple.

This time he heard her. He jumped to his feet, slapping the pistol out of her hand. It flew across the floor to the corner of the room.

"Beth, have you gone mad? What the hell are you doing here?"

"I could ask the same of you."

He smiled an impish grin, "Just having a little fun, that's all."

Beth pointed to the young woman on the floor, crying. "It doesn't look like she's having any fun."

"A man has needs," Douglas argued. "Since you're no help in that territory, I think it's only fair that…"

"Is this the way it's going to be?" Beth cried. "Is this the way it will be after we're married?"

"I don't understand you, Beth. You've lived your entire life on a plantation, and you still haven't learned anything. I love you, and I will never love another woman, it will always be you…my wife." He pointed to the girl, still lying on the floor. "I own these people. They are my property. They are just things. I ride more than one horse. I have a favorite, but I do ride other horses. I eat off different plates, drink out of different glasses. They're just things that I use. You will be my wife."

The poor girl on the floor, jumped up, running out the front door in hysterics, holding her torn dress close, to maintain some dignity.

Beth backed away, and was out the door, also.

"Beth, wait, you're being childish!" he shouted, not able to catch up with her, as he still was adjusting his trousers.

When she got to the main house, she hopped into buggy, and rode off. She went so fast, at every turn, some of the food flew out of the back, onto the side of the road. With tears in her eyes, she rode faster and faster till on one particularly sharp turn, the buddy tipped over, falling into a ravine. The leather straps holding the horse in place snapped. The beast ran off in fear.

Struggling to her feet, her mind dazed, she wiped the tears from her eyes. When her sight cleared, she looked to her left. There was the mountain, looming over her.

Nothing made any sense anymore, nothing mattered. Instead of walking down the road, back to the Malum Plantation for help, she started toward the mountain. At the foot of the slope, she looked up, took a deep breath, and began to climb.

She trudged higher and higher with only one goal in mind, to find the cave and find Anthony.

She moved about haphazardly without concern for her well-being. Halfway up the mountainside, her dress was torn by the bushes. There were thin bloody scratches on her hands, arms, neck, and face, caused by brushing into brambles and along rocks. She knew that in time, when she didn't turn up at home, they would become worried. When they found the overturned buggy, they would send a search party out to look for her. She needed to move swiftly.

She had no idea where the cave was or how to find it. She could be walking in circle, for all she knew. Once the sun set, the woods were dark, making travel impossible. Finally, exhausted, she fell to the ground, closing her eyes, she fell fast asleep.

In the morning, waking with the first light, she held no idea where she was. Only for the tilt of the landscape did she know uphill from down. She wandered the full day, going always upward. Everything looked neither somewhat familiar nor unfamiliar, there wasn't much difference. A forest changes its look daily.

One thing she was grateful for was there was no sign of a search party. Knowing her parents, and knowing Douglas, they were sure to be about and not far behind.

Again, as with the first day, the second day was fruitless. When darkness covered the woods, she found a large tree, sat and braced herself against it, and fell asleep.

For three days she wandered near the top of the mountain, searching for the cave. Not having eaten, weakness plagued her.

Looking back down the mountainside, still she saw no sign of being perused.

To make matters worse, it began to rain – hard. In a few moments, she was soaked, her drenched clothes weighting her down. Although, she was finally able to get a drink of water by hold her mouth open to the sky.

In time, even the forest was steeped with water, nearly flooded. The now heavy branches hindered her movement. The grassless areas of dirt now became pools of deep mud.

She stepped into one, sinking to her ankles. Using what little strength she had left, she tried to break free. It was useless. Finally, the only way to move on was to pull her feet out of the muck and mire, leaving her shoes imbedded. Reaching her hands into the bog, she desperately tried to retrieve her shoes. She didn't have the strength, leaving her shoes, moving on, barefoot.

As the sun set and darkness ruled the forest, thunder began to shake the world as flashes of lightning lit it up.

Weak, unable to continue, she fell to her knees, her tears mingled with the rain. She fell forward, facedown in the mud. A hazy humor flooded her, the mind shutting down in a faint.

Her mind filled with visions, not dreams, for it was not a natural sleep. In her vision, she saw faces, black faces, all staring into the sun.

"Stop…!" Beth shouted to them. "Stop it, you'll go blind."

One of the women in the vision turned to her, smiling, "It's you who are blind," she replied in a caring manner.

The vision changed, the faces disappeared. Beth found herself in a dilapidated one-room cabin in the slave quarters. On the floor was the young slave girl that she caught Douglas abusing. The child/woman looked up to her with tear-filled eyes.

"It begins and ends with you," the girl whispered up to Beth. "It begins and ends with each and every one of us."

Just then, Douglas entered. Standing before the girl, he took his belt from his trousers, and began whipping her with it. Standing behind Douglas, Beth couldn't see the girl; she could only hear her screaming. Moving around Douglas, the girl on the floor was in full view. Only, now it wasn't the girl being whipped, it was herself, pleading with Douglas for mercy.

Again, the vision changed. Beth stood before a lovely little cottage, surrounded by a garden and a picket fence. She walked the pathway through the garden to the front door. She didn't think of knocking, she entered. There she found the inside as lovely as the outside. Standing in the center of the parlor was Anthony. There was a peace about him, as he smiled at her.

"Welcome home," he said. "I've been waiting."

"How long have you been waiting?" Beth asked.

"…as long as you have, all my life."

Suddenly, he began to fade away, first transparent, then disappearing. He spoke one last time before he was gone.

"I love you, Beth. Come to me before we turn to gold."

With that, the vision vanished. Beth was thrown into the real world by a bright flash of lightening and the crash of thunder that followed.

Opening her eyes, the earth was dark. Then a flash of lightening gave her a quick, short glimpse of what was before her. It was the mouth of the cave.

She struggled to her feet, walking to the cave. Inside, she could only make her way from the flashes of lightening. Everything was a she remembered it. The pelts on the floor where they slept and made love, the circle of stones where the campfire burned, it was all there.

She fell to her knees. In the circle of stone, all that was left were ashes. She placed her hand down in the center. The ashes were cold. No one had been there for the longest time. She began crying, again.

Chapter Thirty-Five

Turn to Gold

Life became comfortable for Anthony on the Helfer Farm. He'd become close with many of the other workers, not to mention his respect and affection for Mr. and Mrs. Helfer. They turned out to be nearer to his heart than any family.

Only his love and sense of duty gave him the fortitude to leave. After saying good-bye to his newly made friends, he stood at the white picket fence of the Helfer home. Mrs. Helfer handed Anthony a sack full of food for the journey.

"Man does not live by bread alone," she said, smiling. "See that thee say thy prayers everyday."

"I will, ma'am," Anthony nodded, holding the sack to his chest.

Jacob took hold of Anthony's hand, shaking it as he spoke, not stopping till he'd finished his full thought. "Go with God, my son. The way is narrow, stay to the narrow path. Remember, if thou ever need a friend, here stand two. If thou art hungry, if thou need shelter, if thou art naked, you have a home." He stopped shaking Anthony's hand.

"Thank you, sir," Anthony said with great emotion.

With that, the Helfers turned, entering their home, not waving or giving him one last look. They'd said their piece. They were leaving it in God's hands.

****

Anthony paid little attention to surroundings. It was as if a magnet was lodged in his brain, drawing him to the Malum Plantation. He was lost in thought, yet only three images filled his brain, Emma, Antoinette, and Beth, the three people who meant the world to him. He would gladly lay down his life for any one of them.

The plan was to save Emma and Antoinette. The meeting on the mountaintop with Minty would be in less than a week. He could visualize in his mind what he had to do, and how he was to do it.

As for Beth, he had no answers. Far as he could tell, Beth was a dream, a fairytale, a love affair to remain unfulfilled.

Looking about, he began to recognize the terrain. He was close. He planned to find the cave, rest, and make his way to Malum Plantation in the morning.

Traveling up the mountainside, he could see the cave off in the distance. When he got to it, he stood silently, motionlessly, in front of the mouth. He dreaded entering. It would remind him of Beth, and he knew what pain came with that remembrance.

A campfire would be needed. He gathered some dry stick from the ground, carrying them in his arms. He entered the cave.

Inside, there was little light. When his eyes adjusted, he moved to the circle of stones, placing the firewood in the center. That's when he became aware of someone on the ground next on his right. At first, it frightened him, till he realized they weren't moving. He reached out, turning them onto their back.

"Beth…!" he shouted, his voice echoing off the walls and ceiling.

She did not respond.

"Beth…Beth," he repeated, taking her into his arms.

Slowly, her eyes opened. A weak smile appeared, when she recognized him. "Anthony," she moaned, falling into a swoon.

He built a fire, holding her close. "It's all right, I'm here, now."

****

The next few days, he feed and nursed her. It didn't take long for her to regain most of her straight. It was like old time, going for walks, talking, laughing, and making love.

He told her where he'd been, what happened, and what his plans were. "I have to go down to the plantation. I've vowed to save Emma and Antoinette. I only have a couple more days till when I have to meet with Minty."

A fear took hold of Beth. It was a miracle they were together, and they both knew it. She wanted nothing to ruin it, yet here he was planning to put it all on the line. Then shame crept over het. She knew what he planned to do was right. Besides, she loved him because of the man he was, and this was what made him that man.

"Is there anything I can do?" Beth asked.

"Yes, there is. You can stay here and wait for me. Knowing you're safe means the world to me. It will make what I have to do easier. Will you do that for me?"

She nodded. "When will you be leaving?" she asked, fearing the answer.

"With the first light…"

"Then we at least have tonight."

"Why do you say that?" he asked. "You make it sound so final. There is nothing in this world that can separate you from my love."

He kissed her gently, guiding her to lie next to him. That night, they didn't eat, nor did they feed the fire, letting the wood burn out, the flames dwindling till darkness filled the world. They made love till they fell asleep in each other's arms.

****

They naturally woke at the same moment, early morning, before the sun peered over the horizon.

"I have to go," he whispered, standing up, getting dressed. "No, don't get up. It'll be easier if you just let me leave."

Once he was dressed, he reached down, arranging the pelts covering her naked body. They kissed. He rose, without looking back, he left.

Beth remained under the furs, already missing Anthony. The first rays of the morning sun cut through the darkness of the cave.

The next moment, Anthony came running into the cave. His face was wriggled with fear and his eyes were wide. He rushed to her, falling to his knees.

"Anthony…?"

"Do you love me?"

The question took her off guard.

"Do you love me?" he repeated.

"Of course, I do."

"Do you trust me?"

"With my life…" she responded.

"Do what I tell you without question."

"Anthony, I…?"

"Don't say a word."

"Anthony, you're scaring me."

"Trust me," he said; reaching for a length of rope, he began to tie her hands behind her.

"Anthony…?"

"Trust me," her repeated.

Once her hands were bound, he bound her feet, as well. Then, using a strip of clothe, he gagged her mouth. Finally, she was bound and gagged, naked. He stood up.

Without warning, men from the plantation rushed into the cave. They were led by Monk and Douglas. They were carrying rifles.

Before Anthony could make a move, Douglas rushed him, ramming his rifle butt into Anthony's stomach. When Anthony bent over in pain, Douglas came up with his rifle butt into Anthony's face. Anthony went limp, falling to his knees.

"Get him out of here!" Douglas shouted to the others.

Monk nodded to his men. Two of the men took hold of Anthony, dragging him out of the cave.

"All of you, out of here!" Douglas ordered.

"All right, boys," Monk said, leaving the cave, followed by the others.

Alone, Douglas knelt down beside Beth. She was crying.

"Now, you understand?" he questioned, not expected an answer. "I understand it wasn't your fault. You had nothing to do with this. It was against your will. He kidnapped you, and raped you."

He reached over removing the gag from her mouth.

"What will you do with him?" was the first words out of her mouth.

"Don't worry, my love," Douglas said. "You will be revenged. He will be killed. Just not now, I'd like to kill him, now, but you know how my father is. 'Never waste an opportunity to put fear into them', he always says. He will be executed for all to see."

Douglas untied her. He held her close. "Now, you understand," he repeated. "Now, you understand that when I was with that slave girl, it was nothing. Just like this is nothing. I'm not angry, I'm just sad that you had to go through this."

Douglas' arms around her were like a caged, growing smaller with each second, tightening around, and squeezing the life out of her. At that moment, Beth wanted to die. If not for the though that Anthony would need her, she would have.

Douglas stood up, looking around, he found her clothes, picked them up, and handed them to her.

"Here, get dressed," he said, backing away.

Beth took up her clothes. She looked at Douglas, hoping he would leave the cave and let her dress in privacy. Except, he didn't, instead, he folded his arms, watching her every move, enjoying the moment.

When she was dressed, he placed his arm around her, guiding her out of the cave. Outside, the men were waiting, two men holding Anthony, his hands now tied behind his back.

Her eyes met with Anthony's. So much was said between the two of them, in that moment. She wanted to scream of her love to the world. Only, his eyes told her not to, and that he understood. He wanted her to be safe. He was sacrificing himself for her. She needed to have faith and believe that somehow what he said was true. "There is nothing in this world that can separate you from my love."

"All right, boys," Monk announced.

They started down the mountainside, Monk up front, followed by two men guiding Anthony, then the others, and finally, Beth and Douglas, his arm tightly around her.

As they moved downward, Beth never took her eyes off the back of Anthony's head. For some strange reason, she remembered the dream she once had of Anthony. When he said, "I love you, Beth. Come to me before we turn to gold". Even stranger was that a part of her, now, understood what that meant.

Thirty-Six

Blood Doesn't Wash Away

Only small slivers of light came through the cracks of the toolshed. They emptied it of all the tools, threw Anthony in, and locked the door. He sat on the floor, waiting.

Midday, the heat rose in the shed, causing sweat to pour from Anthony. Without water, his tongue swelled, the back of his throat was dry. His body ached, badly. Before they shoved him inside, Monk and his men took turns beating him. They laughed as they punched and kicked him. In the dark, he was unable to see how bad the wounds were, though he could taste blood. Three of his teeth were coming loose, barely remaining in place.

"I can't wait to see ya hang," a voice oozed through the planks of the shed door. "Ya made me look bad. But now, you're gonna get yours."

It was Monk, letting out all his anger.

"What made ya think ya could touch a white woman?"

"She's not a white woman…she's Beth," Anthony answered back.

The response flew clear over Monk's head.

"I can hardly wait for ya to hang. See ya in the mornin'."

Anthony heard Monk's boots shuffling across the grave, fading away.

Nearing the evening, when the heat of the day was subsiding, Anthony found little relief. He was thirsty, hungry, and tired, though he couldn't sleep.

A young woman's voice seeped through the door, "I can't stand to see a body suffer."

Anthony looked down at the space at the bottom of the door and the ground. A plate slipped under. It was a woman's hand, young, black, and hard worked. On the plate was a fired egg, a piece of bread, and the lid from a jar filled with water.

"Ya need to eat it right now. I gotta get the plate back. If they find anythin' missin', it'll mean my hide."

Anthony didn't need to be asked twice. He swallowed the water in two gulps. It was a relief to the back of his dry throat. He placed the egg on top of the slice of bread, and then slipped the plate back to her.

"Thank you," he whispered. "God bless you."

"I just can't stand to see a body suffer." With that, Anthony heard her walk away.

After the sun went down, the inside of the shed was dark; still, it was a whole lot cooler. Anthony heard heavy footsteps approaching the shed. Someone knocked on the door, which was odd. It wasn't as if he were going to answer, or invite the person in.

"Anthony, it's me, Douglas, your brother," Douglas said this laughing, as if he told some bizarre joke, and perhaps it was.

"What do you want?" Anthony asked.

"Nothing," Douglas responded. "I've got everything that I want. And once you're out of the way, there'll be no denying it. It's one of the oldest stories in human history, sibling rivalry. It goes all the way back in the Bible to where Cain killed Able. Only this time it turns out right. This time the young brother destroys the older brother. And it's you who'll have been marked."

"She loves me, not you," Anthony countered, knowing that's what this was all about, knowing there was nothing Douglas could say to hurt him.

"She will forget you," he shouted back.

"You'll never really know that, will you?" Anthony replied.

Douglas turned and marched away.

Anticipation of the morning, Anthony was unable to sleep. Still, he lied flat on the ground with his eyes closed, resting. He sat up, when he heard footsteps.

Anthony thought it strange that no one paid much attention to him all his life, and now, on the last night of his life, the interchange was constant.

"Anthony, are you awake? It's your father."

Anthony didn't answer. Was Fergus playing with him?

"I need to talk with you."

"Go ahead, I'm listening," Anthony replied.

"I want you to know that I don't hate you."

It was then Anthony realized Fergus was drunk.

Fergus continued, "I don't, I really don't. But this will be better for all concerned. I made many mistakes when I was young, and I'm afraid you're one of them. Perhaps, when you're gone, I can find some peace."

"So, you don't ask for forgiveness, you just destroy all the evidence?" Anthony reacted bitterly. "You're forgetting one thing. When I'm gone, there'll still be Emma, and your grandchild, Antoinette."

This seemed to have derailed Fergus; he went silent for a long time.

"I never thought about that," Fergus admitted. "You're right. Something will have to be done."

Fear seized Anthony by the throat. His cold remark, his slip of the tongue may cost Emma and the baby their lives.

Anthony pleaded, "I've done you wrong. I know that. But, they have never done anything wrong to you. For God sake, man, they're your flesh and blood."

"It's all my fault," Fergus declared. "See what trouble your births have caused. It would have been better, if none of you would have been born. I wash my hands of all of you."

"Blood doesn't wash away," Anthony added. "God knows, God see, and he'll remember."

Fergus had no answer to this. His only defense was to ignore it, forget it, and walk away.

Anthony tried kicking the door down, nothing. Then he spent at least an hour, pushing his feet against it, nothing.

It was late, surely after midnight. Anthony didn't hear anyone approach, nevertheless, someone was on the other side of the door. They were fiddling with the lock.

"Who's there?" Anthony asked.

There was no response, only the sound of someone tinkering away. Anthony heard the sound of nails being pulled out of wood, and then the sound of the lock falling to the ground with a thud. The door opened. The three-quarter moon lit up the night. Anthony was already standing, prepared for whoever was on the other side of the door.

"Simon?" Anthony gasped with surprise.

"Keep it down," Simon said, gesturing for Anthony to follow him.

When they got out of earshot of the main house, at the edge of the slave quarters, Simon turned to Anthony.

"Emma is my daughter and Antoinette is my granddaughter. Yes, I know all about Massa Malum. But I was there the night Emma was born. I walked the floor with her when she cried in the night. I spoon-fed her, and changed her. I picked her up when she fell. I've loved her all her life, and she loves me. I am her true father, not Malum.

"Now that Colby is gone, I see the signs. It is not going to get better for Emma. It is going to get worse. Something has to be done, but I'm too old to do anything. You're still young, you can. I know you still love your sister."

Anthony nodded, even thought the word "sister" cut into his heart like a sharp knife. "Yes, I love them both. I was planning to take them away, when I was captured."

"Now, you have the chance," Simon told him. "Don't tell me what your plans are. They may try to get me to talk. It'll be best I don't know. Go, they're still living in the same house they lived in when Colby was alive. Go...quickly. God bless you."

The urgency in Simon's voice sent shutters up and down Anthony's body. There was no time for words. It was time to act.

Anthony backed away slowly, and then turned, running through the slave quarters. It was late, and no one was awake, yet. When he got to the shack, he tiptoed onto the porch, gently knocking on the front door. There was no answer, so he tried, again.

"Who is it?" Emma's timid voice called out.

It took him a moment. "It's me, Anthony."

Slowly, Emma opened the door. They stood silently staring at each other. Both had a strong urge to fall into the other's arm, but they fought the feeling, believing it best.

"You escaped?" Emma exclaimed.

"I need to come in, Emma."

She moved aside for him to enter.

"If you escaped, why aren't you on the run? Why are you here?"

"I've come to take you with me."

"Anthony, you know we can't."

"Not in that way, Emma. I'm taking you to the Underground Railroad. They'll take you north, to someplace safe."

"Anthony, I don't know."

"It's the only way, Emma."

She nodded in agreement. "I need to say good-bye to my parents."

"There's not time for that. I've already talked with your father. He understands. We have to leave this very minute."

A look of resolve came over Emma's face. She quickly dressed, packed a few things in a sack, and then took the sleeping baby up in her arms.

"We're ready," she announced.

As soon as they got to the edge of the slave quarters, baby Antoinette woke, and began to cry, loudly. The child's bawling woke folks. Then the dogs in the kennel started to bark. This would set wheels in motion.

When they entered the fields, Anthony took hold of Emma's arm. "We need to run. Can you run?"

Emma nodded.

They ran through the field toward the woods. Anthony looked back. It was as he feared. Lights were coming on at the main house and where the overseers slept. They needed to run faster. Anthony took hold of the sack in Emma's arm, tossing it aside. She said nothing, knowing it was slowing them down. Then he took Antoinette from her. They could run faster, now.

When they got to the woods, the sound of the dogs wasn't far off. Running up the mountainside was difficult. Many times, Anthony took hold of Emma's arm, having to drag her to move faster.

The men and dogs were in the field making their way to the woods. All of a sudden, there was the sound of dogs yelping and crying. Something was wrong. Something or someone was hurting the dogs. Whatever it was, it was giving them precious time to gain a lead.

The unmistakable voice of Monk came from below. "Don't just stand there, shoot the bastard!"

The next instant, the sound of gunfire exploding sounded, and then echoed off the mountainside.

Emma and Anthony looked back in wonder. Then they heard a woman's voice coming from the field. "Simon…Simon…no!" she cried. It was Cora's voice.

It was then they understood. Simon had attacked the dogs, in hopes of slowing them down. He sacrificed himself for them.

There was no time to morn him. They could do that later. For now, the only thing that matter was that they kept moving.

Thirty-Seven

Mingled As One

Simon's body lay on the table. Folks came, paying their respects. Cora sat in a chair, next to him, holding his hand, crying.

"So sorry for your loss," they said. "If there's anything that you need, don't hesitate to ask," they said. The kitchen was cluttered with food, offerings from neighbors. Eating was the last thing on Cora's mind.

In the evening, after everyone left, and Cora was alone, the door opened, Monk entered, holding his hat in his hand. Four of his men stood behind him.

"Sorry about ya loss, Cora, but ya know what has to be done."

Cora looked up at him through tearful eyes. She knew what he meant. It was customary on the Malum Plantation for all deceit slaves to be buried within twenty-four hours of their death. But there was never any grave, nor was there a cemetery. They buried the bodies in the empty field, which would go without crop for a season. This was to give the earth time to rest and replenish. It was believed that the body would decompose, giving needed nourishment to the soil. So, even in death, a slave served the pleasure of the Massa, as fertilizer.

Cora jumped to her feet, taking the limp body up in her arms. "Don't you touch him!" she cried, her face muffled in Simon's neck.

"Don't give us a hard time, Cora. Ya know the rules."

She turned her head to look at Monk. "It's late. Y'all ain't gonna start diggin' in the middle of the night. Can't you just let me have one more night with my husband," Cora pleaded.

Monk thought about it for a minute. She was right; it was late. They would only carry the body to the field and wait till the morning to bury him.

"All right, Cora. But we'll be back first thing in the mornin'."

"Thank you, sir...thank you," Cora murmured through her tears. "Just a few more hours, that's all I need."

****

Everyone knew Toddy wasn't very bright. Even the slaves laughed at him, behind his back. Still, he was as faithful as a hound dog, willing to obey any command without question. Only, he wasn't much good at thinking on his feet, or off his feet, for that matter.

It was the middle of the night when Toddy pounded on Monk's door.

"What the hell is it now, Toddy," Monk grunted, his eyes half shut, one hand holding up his trousers. "Aren't ya supposed to be patrolling?"

"There's somethin' wrong, Monk. I went to check the barn, and one of the horses is missin'."

Monk dressed and followed Toddy to the barn.

It was true. After checking, it was certain one of the horses was missing. Not one of the better horses, but one of the workhorses, a large strong beast.

Outside the barn, Monk wondered what to do, considering all his options.

Toddy raised his arm, pointing off into the distance. "Look!"

Monk turned to see a bright glow on the horizon. It was large, not a campfire.

"That's where the old church was!" Monk said.

"Maybe, the church is on fire?" Toddy asked.

"That's impossible. It burned down a long time ago," Monk replied, as he ran off to gather some of his men.

They were all armed and ready for the unexpected, when they reached the site of the old church.

On top of the exact spot the church once stood, upon the ashes of the burned down church, was a large fire made up of large logs. Placed atop of the burning wood was the body of Simon Tucker.

Cora stood close to the fire, staring into the flames. The missing horse was off to the side. She obviously used the beast to cart the body to the site, as well as gathering large logs for the fire.

Thankfully, the church site was in a large clearing. The surrounding forest was not close enough to catch fire, although, there was always the chance of flying sparks making their way to the woods.

The blaze was getting larger, easily seen for miles. The men could feel the heat of it on their faces. They could only image what it was like for Cora who stood only less that a yard from it.

There was nothing they could do. It was too late. The fire was beyond being put out. There was nothing left to do but watch it burn.

There came a point in time were it became impossible to tell the burning logs from Simon's body. The flames consumed everything equally.

"Cora! Step away from the fire," Monk shouted, uneasy about getting to close, the heat like the noonday summer sun on his face.

The horse, though far from the flames, was beginning to get skittish. Monk ordered one of his men to take the best back to the barn.

"Cora!" Monk shouted, again.

It was if she'd gone deaf, dumb, and blind to the world. Only the flames of her husband's funeral pyre appeared real to her.

"Cora, I'm warning ya!" Monk called out to her.

Again, she was oblivious to the world, save for the flames.

Suddenly, a gunshot blast shattered the air. The bullet hit Cora square in the chest. Her head flew back, and her body tumbled forward into the inferno. Her large full skirt caught fire in seconds.

Monk and the men turned to look behind them to see where the gunshot came from. They looked just in time to see Fergus Malum lowering his rifle. His son, Douglas, was at his side.

"You are an absolute waste of time," Fergus told Monk.

"Sorry, sir," Monk said, knowing that any argument of defense would only dig a deeper hole.

When Cora's body hit the fire, it set off sparks into the sky. What they feared the most, happened. One of the closer trees to the clearing caught fire. It was just the branches, but it could lead to something worse.

"Get some of the men to ride back and bring us some axes to chop down that tree, before it gets out of hand," Fergus ordered Monk.

Less than a half hour later, the tree was cut down. It crashed down onto the fire, causing other sparks to fly. More trees caught fire, and needed to be cut down.

In time, they got the fire contained. Fergus had the men dig a trench around the area, to make sure it remained enclosed.

Two men were assigned to watch over the fire till it was completely consumed. It took three days to burn out fully.

In the end, there was nothing but a heap of grey ash, the universal end to everything. Ashes, ashes, all fall down.

There was no way to tell the ashes apart. The ashes of the logs, the church, and the bodies of Cora and Simon mingled as one.

Thirty-Eight

No Words Were Said

They kept Antoinette wrapped in pelts. Summer was coming to an end. The cave was becoming cooler, especially during the night.

Emma and the baby seldom left the cave. Anthony went out only long enough to fetch water, wood, or to hunt.

It was an odd time for them, awkward and uncomfortable. It was obvious they both wanted to talk, and needed to. Only, neither Emma nor Anthony dared, as if a single breath could topple everything. It was best to say nothing. It felt safe.

Finally, late in the night, while the baby slept, and the fire died down, Emma found the courage to speak.

"Do you hate me?" Emma asked.

"Hate you? Why would you think that?"

"I don't know. I just don't want you to hate me."

"I can never hate you. I love you," Anthony replied.

"Love...?" Emma questioned aloud. "Love can change."

"No...love never changes."

"Then what changed?" she asked.

Anthony knew the answer, they both knew it. He searched deep within for the words.

"It was just never meant to be," he said, knowing it was a poor answer, the instant he said it.

"You know," she whispered, "Sometimes I wish there wasn't a God. And sometimes I wish he'd just leave us alone. And then after I think these thoughts, I fall to my knees and ask for forgiveness. I just don't..."

Anthony remained silent. He understood how she felt. He knew there were no words to such statements.

"Get some sleep," Anthony said as he put his head down. "We have to get up early. It's not a far journey, but it's a rough one."

Emma settled down to sleep. "I love you, Anthony," she softly called out, her eyes closed.

It took him a moment. "I love you, too."

****

Before the sun rose, Anthony woke Emma. After she nursed Antoinette, they were ready to go.

"You see that mountain up ahead," Anthony asked, pointing. "We have to make it down into the valley, and then up again to the summit. If we move quickly, we can make it in time to meet the Underground Railroad."

Anthony carried Antoinette, as they climbed down to valley, the descent was a steep one. More than a few times, Emma lost her balance, falling to her knees.

"Are you all right?" he asked.

"I'm fine, don't worry about me, you just keep moving."

When they reached the valley, where the footing was better, Emma carried their daughter.

As they walked, they remained silent. It wasn't till they were at the foot of the mountain, when Anthony took Antoinette into his arms, that Emma asked what was on her mind.

"You love her, don't you?"

Anthony looked at her strangely, as he took hold of Antoinette.

Emma continued, "The woman they said you kidnapped. You love her?"

Anthony didn't answer. He just looked at her, as he secured his grip on Antoinette, holding her to his breast.

"I thought so," Emma proclaimed.

"How would you know that?" he asked.

"I know you," she said. "So, what are you going to do about it?"

"Nothing, what can I do? It's the same as you and me. It was just never meant to be."

****

At the summit of the mountain, they were able to see far in every direction. Behind them, they could see the Malum Plantation off in the distance. Before them, more peaks and valleys, as far as the eye could see.

"They're not here," Emma stated.

"Don't worry; she'll be here."

"She...?" Emma questioned in surprise.

After waiting an hour, they saw Minty making her way up the mountainside to them – the old woman and her donkey.

When Minty reached them, it surprised them how energetic she still was, not needed a rest, ready to get on the way.

"This must be the young woman you told me about, and her lovely baby. Nice to meet ya, dear," Minty said, shaking hands with Emma. "My name is Minty; we can talk as we go, but we need to go, now."

Emma looked confused as the old woman started guiding her out of the clearing. "Wait; at least let us say good-bye."

"Make it quick," Minty warned.

Emma, holding Antoinette, moved toward Anthony.

There was one thing on Anthony's mind that he wanted to say to Minty before he forgot. "When you see Mr. and Mrs. Helfer, give them my regards."

"Oh, we won't be goin' that way. In fact, we need to travel around it, keepin' our distance."

"Why, what's wrong?"

"Johnny Rebs," Minty explained. "They came to the farm. There using it for an outpost. Too bad for Jason, they'll steal and ruin everything."

"Didn't he try to fight them?" Anthony asked.

Minty shook her head. "No. Jason's a Quaker. Quakers don't fight back. They turn the other cheek. And when their enemy slaps them on the second cheek, a Quaker only offers the first cheek, again. This insanity continues until either the enemy gets tied of slapping them around or the Quaker falls over dead. Sad to say, it's usually the Quaker who falls dead."

"Then I'm going with you," Anthony announced, "At lease, to the Helfer Farm."

"Why, what do you think you can do?" Emma asked, though it sounded more like a warning.

"I'm not sure, but I won't be turning my cheek."

****

It proved beneficial that Anthony journeyed with them. With his help, they were able to move faster and safer.

Minty pointed north. "That direction leads to the Helfer Farm." She pointed east. "We gotta go that way. Here's where we part. Ya either come with us, or here's where ya say your good-byes," she said to Anthony.

Anthony took Antoinette from Emma, holding the child in his arms. He began to shake and cry, as he kissed his daughter farewell.

"Tell her about me, now and then," he said to Emma.

"I will."

He handed the child back to Emma. Then he put his arms around them both. There was no room to be squeamish, now. They kissed each other through the tears.

Gently, Minty placed her hand on Emma's shoulder, guiding her. Emma backed off, turning and walking away.

No words were said, no good-byes. They would never see each other, again, and they knew it.

Anthony stood watching them fade over the horizon. When they were gone, he turned to the north, the direction of the Helfer Farm, and began walking.

Thirty-Nine

The More the Merrier

Even from a distance, Anthony could tell something was wrong. There was no sound or movements. The Helfer Farm was lifeless.

Stepping onto the property, he found dead bodies in the fields. Approaching the main house and bunkhouse, he found bodies, some of them holding rifles and pistols. It seemed, though the Helfers were pacifists, their workers weren't. Still, they were outnumbered and slaughtered.

Entering the front door of the main house, Anthony's heart sank. The bodies of Mr. and Mrs. Helfer lay on the floor. It was clear they died together. They reached out for each other as they died, for their hands were entwined.

Antony made an inspection of the farm. Everything of value was taken from the main house, including all the food from the kitchen. It was the same with the bunkhouse and the barn.

So many dead bodies, there was no way Anthony could possibly bury them all. He dragged each body one by one into the barn, including the Helfers. With all the dry hay, it took only one match to set the barn ablaze.

Anthony made sure he took possession of a pistol, which he tucked in his belt and a rifle he carried under his arm. He filled his pockets with bullets.

At the edge of the property, footprints in the dirt told the story. There must have been at least a dozen rebels that attached the farm. For some reason, they separated and scattered. The larger group, with a wagon carrying their booty, headed north. Three on horseback, rode south. And three on foot, were walking due east, in the same direction that Minty, Emma and the baby, would be traveling. Anthony thought it best to follow the eastern trail.

****

"I say we kill the old woman. She ain't no good to us," one of the rebels said to the other two.

"What about the donkey?" said another.

"Ya ever eat donkey, it ain't good, but it's better than starvin', "the first replied.

"What about the girl?" asked the second.

"I can think of a lot of things we can do with the girl," laughed the first.

"But she got a baby," the third soldier added.

"How the hell do ya think she got a baby?" the first laughed even louder as he walked toward Emma. "I like a woman with experience." He stood before Emma, grabbing her by the waist. "Why don't ya put that baby down, and let's get friendly."

"Vic, ya sure is somethin' else," the second laughed. "Ya don't care who ya doin' it to, as long as ya doin' it."

"What's the matter, Bill? Ain't ya never had no dark meat, before?"

"Vic, ya sure is somethin' else."

"What about ya, Dole?" Vic asked the third soldier.

"I say we shot the old woman, first. I ain't doin' nothin' with those sad cow eyes lookin' at me."

The other two laughed.

"Well, I like an audience," Vic said. "I perform better with an audience." He stepped closer to Emma. "Now, are ya gonna put that baby down, or am I gonna have to take it from ya?"

Emma turned, giving Antoinette to Minty.

All this time, Anthony was in the nearby bushes, watching it all, wondering what would be the best course of action. When he thought of a plan, he waited for the best time to strike. It would have to be when all three men were occupied. Yet, Anthony knew he needed to act before it got too far.

"So, where were we?" Vic said, looking to Emma. "I know, it's show time. I want ya to take off your clothes."

Emma looked at him blankly.

"Ya know what I'm sayin'. Now, ya want to see that old lady get shot, ya just keep starin' at me like that. Now, do what I say."

Vic backed up to get a better view. He folded his arms before him, as if he were inspecting cattle. The other two stood next to him, watching. Anthony was just about to jump into the clearing, when Dole began complaining about Minty.

"Make the old woman turn around. She's ruining it," Dole said.

"No!" Vic demanded. "I want her to look. I like when she looks." Vic pointed to Minty. "Ya watch this, old woman, and learn your place, ain't never too late to learn somethin'."

He focused his attention back to Emma, as did the other two. This was what Anthony waited for.

In tears, Emma undid the button on her blouse. They trembled as she took it off her shoulders, letting it fall to the ground.

"Go on, now the bottom," Vic ordered.

Emma undid her skit, dropping it to her the ground at her feet. Her undergarment still kept her modestly covered.

"Keep goin'," Vic insisted.

Her entire body was shaking. The three rebel soldiers were completely spellbound, their eyes running up and down her body.

Anthony sprang out of the bushes, into the middle of the clearing. He stood in front of Emma, aiming his rifle at the three men.

"Shows over, boys," Anthony asserted.

"Hold on!" Vic shouted. "We were just havin' a little fun. We weren't plannin' on do any harm."

Anthony looked at the three men in disbelief.

"Emma, get dressed." Anthony said, still holding his aim.

Emma didn't think twice. She so desperately wanted to feel safe and sound, once more. She was back in her clothes, in a flash.

With his hands raised high, Vic approached Anthony.

"Can't we talk about this?" Vic asked.

"There ain't nothing to talk about," Anthony answered back, gritting his teeth.

Emma rushed, taking Antoinette from Minty, holding the child close to her. In that moment of transfer, the baby began to cry. Anthony took his eyes off the men for just a second, to see what the matter was. Vic jumped forward, knocking the rifle away, and then his fist came up, catching Anthony hard on the jaw. Anthony fell down on his back. Vic bent down, taking the pistol out of Anthony's belt.

"Who is this black son-of-a-bitch?" Vic shouted at Emma. "He your husband?"

"No, he's my brother," Emma said, feeling the awkwardness of stating it out loud for the first time.

"Ya brother…?" Vic echoed, questioning. "On your knees, boy," he ordered.

Anthony slowly worked his way up, onto his knees.

"Hands on your head," Vic ordered.

Anthony complied.

"Kill the black bastard," Dole shouted at Vic.

"Oh, I'm gonna kill him," Vic said. "But just not yet. I told ya a like an audience. The more the merrier. How's that sound to ya, bubba?" Vic asked, poking his gun in Anthony's face. "Now, back to where we was," Vic announced, looking to Emma.

"Please, don't..." Emma pleaded.

"Give the kid to the old woman, and get back to center stage."

"Please, no, don't..." Emma repeated.

"Listen, ya gonna do what I say. Now, ya could do it before I shoot bubba's brains out or after. It's up to y'all."

Emma handed Antoinette back to Minty. The poor old woman stood silent, not wanting to make matters worse by saying anything.

Emma stepped forward. Again, she started by unbuttoning her blouse.

Vic kept the pistol aimed at Anthony, although, his eyes were focused on Emma, as were the eyes of the other two soldiers.

Suddenly, a gunshot blasted through the air. The bullet hit Vic's hand, sending the pistol several feet away, his hand spraying blood over Anthony.

Three Union soldiers stepped into the clearing from three different directions, aiming their rifles at the three Johnny Rebs.

Anthony recognized them, immediately. It was his three Union soldier friends, John, Sergeant Turner, and Big Jim.

"You can rise, Brother Anthony," Turner announced.

"What the hell is this...three colored soldiers?" Vic shouted, holding his bleeding hand, the other two with their hands in the air.

"That's right, we colored," John answered. "But, I'd say you were colored, also. Only, you look pinkish, where as we are a beautiful coco brown."

He burst into laughter, as did Turner and Big Jim.

Emma took the opportunity to take hold of Antoinette from Minty. Anthony made it back onto his feet.

"Nice to see you again, Minty," Big Jim said.

"You know each other?" Anthony asked, surprised.

Minty stepped forward, hugging Big Jim. "I never thought I'd live long enough to be glad to see you three. I guess if you live long enough and get old enough, you get to see it all."

"You ain't old, Sister Minty," Big Jim said. "You just finely aged."

Again, everyone was laughing, except of course, the three Johnny Rebs.

Sergeant Turner stepped forward, addressing Anthony, Emma, and Minty. "You folks better skedaddle. There are too many Confederates in these parts."

"He's right; we need to get goin'," Minty added.

Now came the near impossible task of saying good-bye, once more. Anthony held Emma and his daughter close.

"Be well, be happy," he whispered in her ear.

Emma cried into his chest, "Go to her. If you love each other, don't let anyone or anything stop you. May you love and be loved."

With that, she broke free of him. Without looking back, she, holding Antoinette, and Mindy walked off, traveling north.

"You best be goin', too," Turner said.

"What about these three," Anthony asked, pointing at the three Johnny Rebs.

"Oh, you don't worry none about them. We'll take good care of them. Now, you skedaddle. Go in peace, my brother."

Heading west into the sunset, about ten minutes later, Anthony heard three gunshots crack and echo across the distance.

Forty

That's Your Decision

The wedding was back on, as was the romance. This was all done without consulting Beth. Dates were set, arrangements made. Everything was as before.

Beth did not give her consent, nor did she protest. Everything was taken out of her hands. She moved about in the world like a ghost.

The least affected was Douglas. He was all smiles and anticipation, always ready to proclaim his love for Beth. He discussed the wedding and marriage plans to anyone who'd listen, except Beth.

As before, the wedding rehearsal was to be a week before the ceremony. The run through went smoother than the first time. Everyone knew their parts. As well, there were no longer any worries of a kidnapping, like the last time. It would all go effortlessly and peacefully. The rehearsal dinner was planned well, food and drink for all.

There was much toasting, speech making, and jokes told at the expense of the engaged couple. None of it fazed Beth. Her mind was miles away and weeks in the past. All she thought about was Anthony.

When she went to freshen up at the main house, in Douglas' room, she half hoped that when she spun around, Antony would be there, like the first time. Only, this time she was alone, truly alone. She began crying.

She went to the window. Looking out she saw something that stopped her from crying. It was a young black girl carrying a bucket of water from the well to the main house kitchen. Beth recognized her immediately. It was the slave girl that she caught Douglas trying to have his way with. What caught Beth's eye and curiosity was the girl was obviously pregnant.

It can't be Douglas' child, Beth thought. After all, it wasn't that long ago, she caught Douglas and the girl together, ruining his advances on the poor girl. Then it struck her like a lightening bolt. *What if that wasn't the first time*, the words echoed in her mind. She could be having Douglas' child?

Beth had to know, she rushed out of the room, down the stairs, and out of the house, stopping the girl before entering the kitchen.

"Excuse me...excuse me!" Beth shouted.

It took the girl off guard. It shook her up so badly, she dropped the bucket of water. She looked down at the spilled bucket on the ground, and began to cry.

"Don't cry," Beth said. "You can always get another bucket."

"If they found out I dropped it, they'll beat me."

"Who'll beat you?" Beth asked.

The girl remained silent.

"What's your name?" Beth inquired. When the girl didn't answer, Beth repeated the question. "What's your name?

"Mary Ann," the girl finally answered.

"Tell me, Mary Ann, are you having a baby?"

"No, Missy, I just gettin' fat."

Beth placed her hand on Mary Ann's stomach.

"Feels like a baby to me," Beth replied. "Who's the father?"

Mary Ann looked at Beth as if she had asked the price of her soul.

"You can tell me," Beth reassured her.

As if he appeared from out of nowhere, Douglas was standing between them.

"What's going on here?" he demanded.

Both women fell silent.

Douglas looked down, pointing to bucket of spilled water. "Did you drop that?"

The girl just looked blankly at the bucket at their feet.

"Picket it up, and get another one," he shouted, slapping her on the side of her head. She tried as best she could to cover from the blow, as she picked up the bucket, and than ran off.

"What is with you, Beth?" Douglas directed his anger at Beth.

"Douglas, tell me…is that girl having your baby?"

Douglas exploded into laugher. "Where do you get the nerve to ask me such a question?"

"I'm the woman who's going to marry you, that's how. You need to be honest, and tell me."

"I don't need to be anything," he barked. "I'll tell you one thing, though. The woman I marry needs to know her place. I don't know what's gotten into you, lately, Beth, and I don't like it. Ever since, you shacked-up with that darkie, you've been on your high horse. Now, I know you couldn't help what happened. So, I forgive you. Now, can we just get on with our lives?"

"That *darkie* is your brother. Oh, yes, I know. Anthony told me all about it."

"So, it's Anthony, now, is it? A wife needs to obey her husband. You better get that bee out of your bonnet."

"What are you going to do about it, beat me?"

Douglas took Beth by the arm, pulling her away from the house. When they got to the large chestnut tree, a few yards from the house, he slammed her against the trunk. He pressed against her with all his strength and weight, looking at her with fire in his eyes.

"The wedding is just one week away, or I swear you'd have two black eyes, already. You're going to learn, here and now, who wears the pants in this family."

He spun her around, pressing her front and face against the tree trunk.

"Don't move," he growled.

He undid his belt, slipping it through the loops in his trousers. He double folded the belt, holdin it in his right hand. With his free hand, he took hold of the hem of her dress, lifting it up to her waist.

"Here, take this, and hold it!" he ordered her to hold her skirt up.

When she didn't move, he slammed her into the tree trunk.

"I said take it!"

Hesitantly, Beth reached behind her, taking hold of the hem of her dress.

"Higher...hold it higher!" he demanded.

She did as he was told.

With one hand, he tore her undergarments off her, exposing her buttocks and the back of her legs.

Pulling his right arm far back, quickly bringing it forward, the belt slapped across her flesh.

She screamed in pain. Douglas pressed her harder against the tree trunk.

"Hold your tongue, or instead of six, I'll give you a dozen."

Beth clinched her teeth together, hard, struggling not to cry out.

Douglas slapped the belt against her rear, five more times. When he was done, her pink flesh was covered with deep red welts.

The pain was hot and sharp. It made her swoon. She fell to the ground.

Douglas, standing over her, put his belt back on.

"Collect yourself, and join the party, again," he spoke down to her.

He began walking back to the party. When he was only a few feet away, he turned to address her. "I'm sorry this happened. I love you, Beth. I pray this never happens again. But then, that's your decision."

Forty-One

A New Season

On the day of the wedding, everyone on both the Harris and Malum Plantations were up early. There were so many details, the clothes, the decoration, flowers, transportation, and food, just to name a few.

Bishop Waltham, who was to perform the ceremony, arrived the day before, staying the night with the Malums. Although he was doing this as for his friendly gesture for Fergus Malum, and wasn't' charging for his services, he sought compensation in other ways.

He arrived with his secretary the night before, just in time for supper. Of course, both men were invited to dinner. Bishop Waltham ate double portions of everything served, as well as devouring a full bottle *Chateau Coutet* Bordeaux, singlehandedly.

After dinner, Fergus and the Bishop retired to the study for cigars and brandy. When offered a cigar, Bishop Waltham took three, one to smoke in the moment, and two for a later date. He also drank enough brandy to make any salty dog of a sailor lose his sea legs.

Late in the night, as everyone slept, Bishop Waltham, not being able to sleep, crept downstairs to the kitchen. There he enjoyed an encore performance of the entire supper, right down to a full bottle of *Chateau Coutet*. It goes without saying, Bishop Waltham was rotund.

At the crack of dawn, Beth and her bridesmaids arrived at the Malum Plantation. They set up camp in one of the guestrooms in the main house. Their main objective was to dress and primp Beth to look the part of a princess. After which time, they would do the same for themselves.

Meanwhile, downstairs in the kitchen, all hell was breaking loose. All the side dishes for one hundred people needed to be prepared, the bread, the salads, the potatoes, and the greens. Three full cows were slaughtered, and then put in pits over coals the night before to slowly cook, timed for the wedding. Food deliveries were constant throughout the day, as were flowers and barrels of whiskey.

Under the supervision of the overseers, slaves busied with setting up the seating for the wedding, as well as the reception, afterwards.

Starting at three in the afternoon, guest began to arrive. By five o'clock all the guests had arrived, each dressed in their Sunday finest. The front porch of the main house was loaded down with gifts for the newlyweds, wrapped in brightly colored paper.

Once their jobs were finished, all overseers and slaves were nowhere to be found.

As with all such functions, nothing ever goes as planned, everything was scheduled for 5 o'clock, it wasn't until 6 o'clock that all the guest were asked to take their seats. The sun was already on its dive below the horizon, which was good, as the air cooled and the light dimmed. Torches were lit. The guest took their seats.

A violinist was hired. He played soft and low, as the ceremony began.

The first out of the main house was Bishop Waltham, dressed in all his priestly glory, he moved slowly and purposely to the head of the crowd, turned and waited.

Then coming up the main aisle were the parents of the bride and groom. First were Mr. and Mrs. Malum, followed by Mrs. Harris, escorted by a young man, Beth's second cousin on her father's side., Each took their place, front row, on their respective sides.

Next were the bridesmaids escorted by the groomsmen. Arm in arm, they parades up to the front, where the ladies moved to the bride's side, forming a line, as the groomsmen did the same on the opposite side.

Unexpectedly, Douglas and his best man appeared, standing next to Bishop Waltham.

The crowed laughed slightly with delight as four-year-old Kristen Ruskin walked down the aisle, tossing rose petals from a basket onto the walkway. Three-year-old Bo Carver marked up the aisle like a soldier, carrying a pillow before him. On was the wedding rings, which he presented to the Douglas and his best man.

The violinist stopped playing, waiting for the crowd to settle down. At first, the guests whispered and murmured, and then eventually all were silent. The violinist began to play the Bridal Chorus.

Everyone stood, turning to look at the main house. Standing on the porch was Beth, escorted by her father. They marched slowly down the aisle, all heads turning, watching their every move.

Beth looked all that was expected of her, a beautiful princess with flowers in her hair, and a bouquet in her hands. There was no expression on her face. Everyone believed this to only be the reaction of a nervous bride.

"Who giveth this woman?" Bishop Waltham asked, aloud for all to hear.

"I do," her father replied, offering Beth's hand to Douglas. He stepped back, taking his place next to his wife. Douglas moved next to Beth, holding her hand.

"You may all be seated," the Bishop announced. He waited for the rumbling to stop. "Dearly beloved, we are gathered here today, in the sight of God, to join this man and this woman in holy matrimony. If anyone objects to this union, let them speak now, or forever hold their peace."

There was a long silence, only the sound of the wind. Inwardly, somewhere within Beth, deep in her heart, she heard Anthony's protesting, "I object!" However, she knew it was never going to happen, and in one sense she was glad. If he were there, they would kill him on the spot.

After letting the appropriate amount of time pass, it was all just a part of the traditional ceremony, no one expect a protest. Bishop Waltham continued.

"Love is patient, love is kind. It does not envy, it does not boast, it is not proud. It does not dishonor others, it is not self-seeking, it is not easily angered, and it keeps no record of wrongs. Love does not delight in evil but rejoices with the truth. It always protects, always trusts, always hopes, and always perseveres."

At this point, as at all weddings, some of the guests began to cry. Most notable were the bridesmaids, and of course, the mothers of the bride and groom. Handkerchiefs waved like flags on the fourth. For this reason, no one took much notice when Beth began to cry. It was expected of a bride to cry tears of joy on her wedding day. Except, her tears were shed for a totally different reason.

Bishop Waltham's words about love struck into Beth's heart like a red-hot poker. Did these words describe the relationship between her and Douglas? Certainly not! They did though; describe what was between her and Anthony. There was nothing she could do, so she cried.

"Doulas Price Malum, do you take this woman, Beth, to be your lawful wedded wife, to live in holy matrimony? To love her, honor her, comfort her, and keep her in sickness and in health, forsaking all others, for as long as you both shall live?"

"I do," Douglas responded.

"And you, Beth Ann Harris, do you take this man, Douglas, to be you lawful wedded husband, to live in holy matrimony? To love him, honor him, comfort him, and keep him in sickness and in health, forsaking all others, for as long as you both shall live?"

It's a sin to tell a lie echoed inside Beth's mind.

"I...I..." she whispered softly, too low for anyone to hear.

Bishop Waltham, figuring it was a bad case of nerves on Beth's part, surmised her mumbling as an "I do".

"Please, present the ring," Bishop Waltham said softly to Douglas.

Douglas looked to his best man, who produced the ring from his vest-pocket, and handed it to Douglas. Taking Beth's hand, Doulas placed the ring on her finger.

"Repeat after me," Bishop Waltham said. "With this ring, I, Douglas, take Beth to be my wife. To have and to hold from this day forward, for better, for worse, for richer or poorer, in sickness and in health, to love and cherish, till death do us part."

Douglas preformed his part word for word. More moans from crying mothers and bridesmaids filled the air.

Douglas reached into his vest pocked. Taking out a larger ring, he handed it to Beth. She stared at it, like it was a snake.

"Repeat after me," Bishop Waltham repeated for Beth. "With this ring, I Beth, take Douglas…"

She remained silent, staring at the ring in the palm of her hand.

Again, thinking it was a bad case of nerves, the Bishop repeated, "With this ring…"

Beth began shaking; the ring fell out of her hand to the ground. Douglas bent down to retrieve it.

Suddenly, one the guest, a gray haired gentleman from one of the neighboring farms, stood on his chair. "Oh my God, look!" he shouted, pointing to the cotton fields. Time froze as everyone stopped what they were doing to look at the fields of the Malum Plantation. They were on fire. Every single plant was ablaze. Not just one field, but all of them. Every square acre was burning. The setting sun was blotted out from the sky by thick black smoke.

At first, everyone was in a panic. Women screamed, some fainted. Men ran aimlessly in circles. Till finally, some sort of order was restored.

Word was sent to the overseers to gather all the slaves and the buckets they could find. Lines of men, guests, overseers, and slaves were formed from water sources to the burning fields. They ran water as fast as they could, some shoveled dirt onto the burning plants. It was a useless endeavor.

Then, as if they didn't have enough to contend with, smoke billowed from the roof of the barn.

Monk ran to the barn, opening the front door, to let out the horses. To his surprise, he found the stalls empty. Someone already had let the horses loose.

They split their forces; some continued running water to the fields, while other formed a line leading to the barn.

Like the fields, it was useless. The dry wood and hay caught fire like a box of matches. In not time, the barn was engulfed in flames, and eventually collapsed. The only thing left to do was to dig a moat around the fields and barn, to keep the fire contained. They worked as fast as they could.

Douglas ran to one of the toolsheds, he entered emerging a few seconds later with a fist full of dynamite. Along with Monk, he rushed to the irrigation reservoir, in hope of flooding the fields. They planted the sticks of dynamite strategically for optimal damage. They lit the fuses and ran as fast as they could for safety.

The blasts were loud, sending dirt and rock high up to the sky and in all direction. The fuses weren't long enough. Douglas and Monk never made it to safety. Both men were struck down by flying debris. Monk was knocked unconscious; in a second he shook himself to his feet, and limped back to the others. Douglas was not so luck. A large rock flew into the back of his head, killing him instantly.

Meanwhile, the floodgates of the reservoir burst open. In less than a minute, all fields were flooded; extinguishing the fire, send an even larger, darker cloud up into the sky. It hovered over the plantation, like a demon from hell.

When Estella Malum saw her son fall, she screamed like a wounded animal. It took all of Fergus' strength to restrain her, stopping her from running out to him. She fell to her knees, at Fergus' feet.

With the flooding, there was nothing left to do, except dig a ditch around the barn, to keep the fire contained. They did this in a short time.

When that was done, everyone stood, exhausted, even the women who had only stood by watching in horror.

With tears in her eyes, Beth's mother approached her. "He's dead…Douglas is dead," she cried.

There was a blank stare on Beth's face that everyone took to be the look of sorrow.

Just when the mood began to calm, and they thought the hardest part was behind them, everything took a turn for the worst.

"Oh, my God, no!" someone shouted.

Everyone turned to see what was the matter. There, with smoke and flames shooting up like a volcano, the main house was on fire.

Fortunately, there was no one in the house. The kitchen staff came out to help with the fire in the fields.

There was nothing left to do, other than stand and watch it burn. Inside, the curtains were flaming like candles. The windows cracked and burst from the heat. The support columns in the front of the house collapsed, destroying the porch.

In time, the fire swallowed it all up, till the house was unrecognizable. Everyone felt the heat on their faces. The wind blew, sending the flames higher. Without warning, the entire building collapsed, looking like an overly large campfire.

Fergus Malum surveyed his kingdom. Everything he own or cared about had been taken away. Gone were his Plantation, his home, his life, and lastly, most precious of all, his son.

Off on the horizon was a speck that no body noticed. Except, Beth, she saw it. She knew what it was. She never took her eyes off it, the speck growing larger as it rushed closer.

Finally, it was clear to all that it was a horseman, galloping toward them, at top speed.

When he was a few yards away, his features became lucid.

"Anthony!" Fergus shouted.

"Anthony," Beth whispered.

It all happened so quickly and unexpectedly, no one did anything to stop him. All they could do was watch.

He rode through the crowd, to Beth. Halting for only a moment, he reached down, pulling her up and onto the horse, sitting behind him. She put her arms around him, pressing the side of her head against his back. She could hear his heartbeat; it was as loud as hers.

With a slap of the reins, they rode off like the wind, in the direction of the forest. The questions no longer mattered. Where would they go? What was in their future? They didn't know; no more than anyone else does.

As they entered the woods, they went slowly. It was fall, a new season. The leaves fell from the trees, on the ground, turning to gold.

THE END

Michael Edwin Q. is available for book interviews and personal appearances. For more information contact:

Michael Edwin Q.
C/O Advantage Books
P.O. Box 160847
Altamonte Springs, FL 32716
michaeledwinq.com

Other Titles in this series by Michael Edwin Q:

Born A Colored Girl: 978-1-59755-478-4
Pappy Moses' Peanut Plantation: 978-1-59755-482-8
But Have Not Love: 978-1-59755-494-7
Tame the Savage Heart: 978-1-59755-5098
A Slaves Song: 978-1-59755-527-5
Fancy: 978-1-59755-540-1

To purchase additional copies of these book visit our bookstore website at:
www.advbookstore.com

Longwood, Florida, USA
"we bring dreams to life"™
www.advbookstore.com

www.ingramcontent.com/pod-product-compliance
Lightning Source LLC
Chambersburg PA
CBHW060353180626
46817CB00008B/2988